Christmas All Year Long

An Anthology of Holly Jolly Tales

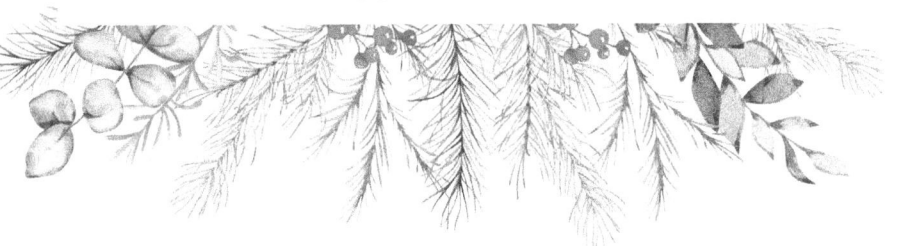

Jan-Carol
Publishing, Inc

"every story needs a book"

Christmas All Year Long
An Anthology of Holly Jolly Tales
Published October 2025
Mountain Girl Press
Imprint of Jan-Carol Publishing, Inc.
Copyright © 2025 Jan-Carol Publishing, Inc.

ISBN: 978-1-970471-00-7
Library of Congress Control Number: On file

You may contact the publisher:
Jan-Carol Publishing, Inc.
PO Box 701
Johnson City, TN 37605
publisher@jancarolpublishing.com
www.jancarolpublishing.com

Dedicated to the talented authors who came together to create an anthology full of holiday magic.

Table of Contents

.

Nannie's

Lori C. Byington

A fresh December snow had fallen overnight, and the early morning sun glistened off the heavily laden Eastern white pines that lined Old Lee Highway. Finally, 1777 Wendover Road was only minutes away "as the crow flies." The familiar drive from Albemarle City, Virginia, to Goodson usually took around four and a half hours, but due to the much-anticipated snowstorm from the west, this trip had taken the Counts family all night to get home.

"Are we there yet?" came a quiet, sleepy voice from the far back of the Woody Mercury station wagon. James, the youngest of the three Counts kids, popped his head up to look over the backseat. "Wow! Look at all the snow!"

James's happy yell roused the two other children, Maggie and Charles, who both shot up from their naps in unison like mini rockets heading to the moon.

"Wheeeee!" squealed Maggie. "Yay! We can ride sleds and build a snowman and make snow cream, and, and..."

"Let's get to your grandparents' first, missy. We still have about

20 minutes to go, and then we have to unload the luggage and the presents before any shenanigans begin," chided their dad, Howard, with a smile. He, too, was excited to see his parents. A new medical office takes time to run, and unfortunately, the family had not been home in a month of Sundays.

Rosa, Mom, turned her head and said sternly, "Ya'll get your blankets and things together so when we get there, we can get everything unloaded quickly. The temperature is about 30 degrees, so bundle up."

The kids did as they were told and settled back down in the backseats for the last few minutes until they arrived at Nannie's.

As the family turned left off of Lee Highway onto Wendover Road, and another left into the drive of Mr. and Mrs. Howard Counts Sr., snow started falling in tiny flakes that looked like dry milk. Howard Jr. teared up at the sight of the white, clapboard house with Williamsburg blue shutters. The white fence along the front of the yard still stood firm.

Momma, a.k.a., Nannie, who had been watching like a red-tailed hawk from the living room window, ran out onto the marble porch, her hands clapping to beat the band with a baby blue kitchen towel slung over her right shoulder.

"Glory be, Howard! The kids are here! Come quick!" she yelled over her shoulder into the house.

As Howard Jr. put the wagon into park, all three kids tumbled out of both back doors, which had been flung open as the car was coming to a stop. They landed in three inches of snow, with no coats, but they did not care. On full run, as fast as they could go, they ran to their Nannie, who had arms already outstretched, waiting to pull the children into her hug. She had a grin as large as the Cheshire cat, and tears of joy slid out of her fierce blue eyes.

"Children! You are finally here!" she cheered as she picked up the smallest, James, with her right arm and hugged the other two older children, Maggie and Charles, with all of her left arm. All three children, muffled in her hug, took deep breaths almost at the same time.

"Nannie! You smell like fried apples and October beans," Maggie exclaimed as she took another deep breath, closed her eyes, and snuggled, happy to finally be at Nannie and Granddaddy's.

"Elizabeth! Let the kids at least put their coats on," came a laughing voice from the front stoop. Granddaddy Howard stood on the stoop with his left hand on his hip and his right hand in his pants pocket in search of a quarter. Not one to show emotion, he grinned slightly and bowed his head to hide tears of relief and joy that his family had arrived home safely.

After a quick sniff, he stated matter-of-factly, "Junior, let me help with the bags. Rosa, you can get the presents," and then he stepped down the wet, marble steps onto the now snow-covered grass.

"Dad! Your Weejuns!" Howard Jr. yelled at Howard Sr.

Howard Sr. raised his eyebrows, looked down at his snowy penny loafers, shrugged his shoulders, and stated, bemused, "Well, I think they are waterproof. I sure do polish these shoes a lot for them not to be."

Nannie grinned at the father-son shoe conversation, reluctantly dropped James to the ground, and released Maggie and Charles so they could go to the car to retrieve their coats and blankets. She waited for Howard Sr. to catch up, and they both followed the grandchildren to help with the unloading.

* * *

Once the kids had bunked into their middle bedroom, and Howard and Rosa were settled in the back bedroom, the whole family went to the living room to relax and sit a spell before supper. The damask, blue couch against the wall, the light blue, winged-back chair in the corner, now hidden by the fresh, Eastern white pine Christmas tree, and the baby grand piano in the corner by the front window were a sight for sore eyes. Howard looked at the fireplace and saw that all the stockings were hung exactly like they always were. Momma and Daddy never had their own stockings out, but all six grandkids' were on full display hanging from the white mantle hovering well above the fireplace. Howard, Rosa, and the kids always loved to come home any time of the year, but Christmas was just more special.

"Nannie! The Christmas tree looks wonderful!" exclaimed Maggie. "All the lights and blue ornaments are so shiny." She stood close enough to look into one large, round, blue ball. "I can see myself!"

Charles and James both jumped up from where they sat on the floor near the fireplace to get closer to the tree to find their own ornaments.

"I want to see myself too!" James cried. He and Charles found other big blue balls and smiled as they saw their noses reflected from the colorful orbs. Charles pulled a silver tinsel strand from a branch, wound it around his finger, and tried to break it. No luck, so he placed the tinsel back on the branch near a light so that it reflected off the silver strand.

"Watch! Don't break the ornaments," Rosa warned. She stood to monitor the excited children as they *oooohed* and *ahhhhed* around the well-lit and ornamented Christmas tree.

Howard Jr. and his dad had been talking about when the other Counts would arrive from King's Port. Howard Sr. relayed that all would be home on Christmas Eve, the next day.

"Momma, the house smells as good as usual," offered Howard Jr. "Do I smell beans and cornbread and coconut cake?"

"Glory be!" Nannie almost screamed as she shot off the couch and skedaddled to the kitchen. "I about burnt the cake!" was heard as she ran through the dining room to her kitchen to save the cake. After loud clanging of an aluminum pan being tossed onto the stove, a relieved voice rang out, "Wheee-ooooh! It's just fine!"

Rosa gave the children a look of *don't break anything* and went to the kitchen to help with supper. The two Howards smiled at each other and cheerfully directed attention to the kids who had, somehow, just noticed the beautifully wrapped presents that were already under the tree.

* * *

Christmas Eve morning dawned bright and sunny. Snow had fallen throughout the night, so another four inches or so of fresh powder blanketed the ground. Nannie had risen earlier than the rest of the family and already had sausage, bacon, and apples frying on the stove, biscuits in the oven, coffee going, and eggs whipped with milk ready to scramble. The clock on the Whirlpool stove showed 8:35 a.m. when a pitter-patter of little feet came into the kitchen. James had risen when he smelled the bacon and was dressed in his *Rudolph the Red-Nosed Reindeer* footie pajamas. Nannie glanced down to see him wiping the sleepy sand out of his eyes with both hands. He yawned as he asked Nannie, "Can I have a piece, please?"

"Why sure! Now, don't tell anyone our secret," Nannie said, smiling. She took a small piece of bacon from the plate where they lay stacked like Lincoln Logs, blew on the piece a little to cool the sizzle, and handed the prize to James.

"Thank you, Nannie!" James mumbled as he stuffed the bacon into his mouth. Still chewing, he put his right pointer finger to his mouth, as if to shush any talk about their secret. Content, James turned around and went to wait in the living room for the others.

Suddenly, someone started pounding on the front door. *BANG, BANG, BANG* on the solid wooden door sounded through the whole house.

"Hello! Is anyone up yet?" came a loud, familiar voice from the front stoop. "Open the door, please! I am about to drop the presents!"

Nannie rushed from the kitchen, wiping her hands on her red and green Christmas apron, and as she got to the front door, Howard Sr., Howard Jr., Rosa, and the other two kids, still in Christmas pajamas, plowed their way from the bedrooms through the hall door into the living room. Charles almost ran into the piano in the corner as Maggie pushed forward like a bull in a China shop.

"The cousins are here!" yelled Maggie, happily.

Grinning from ear to ear, Nannie opened the door to a pile of gifts wrapped in festive colors of the season. Behind the gifts was her other son, Richard, and behind him huddled on the stoop was the rest of the family: Martha, Essie, David, and little Flora. They had driven from King's Port, which was about an hour down Lee Highway.

"Merry Christmas!" yelled the other Counts in unison.

"Ho, ho, ho! Meeeerry Christmas!" responded Howard Jr. as he stepped forward to relieve his brother of some of the packages.

"How were the roads from King's Port?" asked Howard Sr. as he stood back a bit from the door with his hands in his gray, polyester pants pockets.

"Well, not too bad. The trucks were out plowing the snow early, so we left on time as planned," responded Richard. "The house sure smells good, Momma! I am hungry as a bear!"

The other Counts all crowded into the living room, carrying a few bags of luggage. Big hugs and "welcome homes" were passed around the family for a few minutes.

Happy as can be, Elizabeth nodded to the hall door, directing, "Martha, why don't you take your bags to the middle bedroom. The kids can sleep on couches and the floor. We have plenty of pillows and covers. I am sure they won't mind—not that they will sleep with Santa Claus coming tonight."

No one needed to tell them where to go. Martha, Essie, and David carried the luggage through the hall door to the bedrooms, which would be happily full for Christmas Eve.

Little Flora had stopped to admire the Christmas tree, and James went to stand beside her. "Look, Flora, you can see yourself in the big, blue Christmas balls!" he directed, proud to have experienced the fun before his cousin.

Leaning forward as James had directed, Flora giggled, "Oooooh! My nose looks big!"

"Breakfast is ready!" came a yell from the kitchen. "Come before the food gets cold!" Nannie instructed.

Not one of the Counts paused an instant as all went into the dining room to await the blessing before they ate.

"All ready?" asked Howard Sr. "Join hands and let's say our blessing."

After everyone held a hand, big and small, in unison, the family recited: "God is great. God is good. Let us thank him for our food. By his hands we are all fed. Give us, Lord, our daily bread. Amen." Little Flora and James added emphasis to, "AMEN!"

Nannie beamed as the family all went through to get breakfast and then found seats wherever they could. The Poppy Trail China plates were full of bacon, sausage, eggs, biscuits, and fried apples, but Nannie always waited until last to make sure everyone got their fill.

After the breakfast dishes were washed, the leftovers were put in the fridge, and the Howard Counts children had changed from their pajamas, the unanimous decision was made for all to go downtown to shop for last-minute gifts and maybe see Santa at Kress' Department Store. While the other adults got ready to go, Howard Sr. entertained the kids, as usual, with his magic tricks. His most famous trick used a quarter along with anyone's ear.

"Oh! I want to go first, Granddaddy!" Essie squealed excitedly, as she plopped herself down beside him on the blue living room couch.

"Okay. Now, everyone stand back so I can work the magic," Granddaddy instructed.

He reached and took the shiny quarter from his pants pocket and held the magic orb up between thumb and forefinger, just so all could see it was really in his possession. Each child stared intently at the quarter to make sure it was real. After the inspection, Granddaddy took the quarter, still between his thumb and finger. He faced Essie, moved her dark curls aside, and put his hand behind her left ear. With a flourish, quick as a wink, he brought his hand back, rubbed both hands together, and opened them wide. The quarter was gone!

"Whooo! Where did it go?" yelled David and Charles in unison.

"It went into Essie's ear!" Granddaddy answered with a sly grin.

Essie giggled as she felt in her ear and behind her head.

"It's not there, Granddaddy!" gushed Essie in surprise. "Where did it go?"

With another grand flourish, Granddaddy rolled his hands together, put them behind his back on both sides, and then brought both hands forward at once. His fists were closed tight, but when he opened his right hand and faced his palm up, there was the missing quarter.

At this point, Nannie came into the living room and grinned while she announced, "Now, Howard. We are ready to go. Let's get these children in their coats so we can leave."

* * *

Around seven o'clock, after their grand excursion and dinner of steak and gravy, complete with mashed potatoes and peas, all the Counts went to sit a spell in the living room with the Christmas tree. A full day of walking around downtown, shopping, eating lunch at Woolworth's, and a surprise trip to see Santa Claus had plum worn out the six Counts children. Flora yawned first, followed by James, David, Charles, Essie, and Maggie. They were obviously ready for bed, even though the night happened to be Christmas Eve. The elder Counts were tired as well, so they decided to go ahead with their yearly tradition. The Christmas story from the *King James Bible* in Luke 2 was recited by Nannie, and "'Twas the Night Before Christmas" was read by Granddaddy, of course. Without much prodding, the children went off to bed to dream "while visions of sugar plums danced in their heads."

* * *

Christmas morning dawned bright and sunny. The sun reflecting off the snow looked like diamonds and crystals. Nannie was up early, again, preparing Christmas morning breakfast. The warm smell of Pillsbury cinnamon buns with orange icing mingled with the smell of JFG coffee wafted through the house. Nannie always put a maraschino cherry in the center of each bun. Some were red and some were green, and the sauce from the cherries oozed down the bun sides, adding sweetness to the orange. Smells from the kitchen were the perfect waking alarm the family needed. The children, all six, apparently had jumped up at the same time from the bedrooms because they clumped together in a rush to get through the hall door into the living room to see what Santa had left under the Christmas tree. The lights were already lit on the tree, so the blue and silver ornaments were aglow. All were giggling and clapping their hands happily as they looked under and behind the tree for presents that might have their names on them. They were clearly excited for Christmas.

"Come on, Mommie and Daddy!" Maggie yelled impatiently.

"Yes! Santa came!" Essie concurred, yelling louder for emphasis.

The adults slowly made their way from the back and middle bedrooms to the living room. Richard was still tying his robe around him, and Howard Jr. was shuffling to put on his house shoes when they came through the door to witness their children impatiently jumping around.

"Quiiiiit. Settle down," Howard Jr. told the children. "Wait until your Nannie and Granddaddy get out here."

Richard responded, "Essie, David, and Flora, you all listen to your Uncle How."

The minute the dads had their say, the moms, Nannie—with her Christmas apron on—and Granddaddy all wandered into the living room with big smiles on their faces. Granddaddy sat in his place in the blue and off-white, wing-backed chair. The chair had been moved to make way for the tree, so he was a tad hidden by branches.

"Merry Christmas!" Nannie laughed and clapped her hands. "Let's see what Santa has brought you children!"

Howard Jr. responded in a deep voice, "Meeerrry Christmas! Ho, ho, ho!"

"Merry Christmas, everybody!" offered Richard. "Children, go sit so we can hand out the presents."

Without hesitation, all six Counts grandchildren plopped themselves onto the carpet like frogs on lily pads. Each one was spaced apart strategically so Nannie could hand out the gifts without stepping on anyone. After retrieving much-needed coffee from the kitchen, Howard, Rosa, Richard, and Martha sat down on the couch. The ripping of Rudolph, Coca-Cola Santa Claus, Frosty the Snowman, and various other Christmas wrapping papers and bows sure caused a ruckus. The stockings were still on display on the mantle, but the children paid no mind. Those could wait until the important presents had been ransacked.

Granddaddy sat watching his brood, and Nannie stood smiling near the dining room entryway. The black and gold clock on the mantle struck 9:00 a.m. with a *bonnnnngggg*. Christmas had arrived at Nannie's.

Mr. Santa

Colleen De Simone

Violet huffed as she struggled to reach the zipper on the back of the dress. She paused to blow her bangs out of her face and glance in the changing room mirror. Even before being fully zipped, the gown was gorgeous. Satin, in a deep, Christmas-tree green with golden, delicate chain shoulder straps. It clung to her body in perfect form with a thigh slit almost right to her hip that would turn every head in the room. She felt elegant. Sexy. Poised.

Unfortunately, none of those feelings came with a check, and the price tag on the dress was the type that would garner a whistle.

Still, she'd be damned if the only perk of working extra hours at the department store during the holidays was her modest—and that's putting it nicely—paycheck. After-hours fancy clothes try-ons were one of her favorite ways to put a little seasonal joy back into days filled with hurried customers, unsupervised children, and attitudes that warranted frequent deep breaths and fake smiles.

Another reach for the zipper confirmed that putting on this dress was a two-person job. With one hand at her spine to hold the fabric together, Violet made her way out of the dressing room in search of assistance.

"Gemma? A little help?"

The dressing rooms boasted their own alcove with walls that curved slightly around the entrance, offering a bit of a reprieve from the open floors of the rest of the store. The center of the space fit a small desk for the attendant, and there were two floor-length mirrors on either side. Violet poked her head around the edge of the wall, scanning a sea of clothing racks and displays for Gemma's cute ginger space buns.

"Hello?" Violet whispered harshly. *Ugh. She would run off in the middle of me trying on clothes.* She took a few steps forward. She was mostly sure that the rest of the staff had gone home for the night. Still, did she want to parade through the store adorned in a dress almost entirely held closed by her thumb and forefinger? Probably not.

Damn. I really wanted to get a cute picture in this. Violet sighed and resigned herself to putting it back on the rack. *Oh well.* At least she'd gotten to try on a few other gowns. This one was the last.

A throat cleared beside her, deep and low. Violet spun around, angling her back to the wall so as to hide her zipper predicament.

If she was looking for joy…she doubted much could brighten things up like the man now leaning against the archway into the dressing rooms. Whatever she'd been thinking or planned to say left her brain as quickly as it had come. She stared, dumbfounded, at dark chocolate eyes resting below bouncy curls of black hair accented by silver strands in perfect proportions. Full lips flashed a smirk in her direction, giving rise to high cheekbones and arched eyebrows.

"Need some help?" The richness in his voice was so smooth and distracting, she almost didn't comprehend what he said. But when he cocked his head and took a step in her direction, she quickly snapped out of her ridiculous stupor.

"What are you doing here?" She donned her typical work tone and planted her free hand on her hip. "We closed 45 minutes ago. You'll have to wait till tomorrow to get your holiday shopping in." Gorgeous or not, it was way past the time when she was supposed to have to put up with customers.

Mr. Sexy held his hands up in defense. He backed away quickly, giving her a wide berth that she greatly appreciated. "Apologies, I didn't realize." He paused to glance around the store. "Guess the emptiness should've given it away, huh?"

He chuckled and Violet couldn't tell if he was laughing at himself or at her.

"I'll get out of your hair and let you get back to..." He gestured at her dress, his eyes traveling down the floor length gown in a way that sent pleasant shivers across her skin. She hoped to hell she wasn't blushing, but when his eyes flicked back to her face and the corners of his lips twitched, she figured that hope was entirely in vain. "Back to your evening," he finished softly.

Then he turned on his heels with one hand in his pocket and strode towards the store's exit. Violet leaned to the side to watch him go, shamelessly eyeing the way his jeans curved around his backside and down long, muscled legs.

She chewed her lip a moment. He had offered to help zip up her dress, hadn't he? She scanned for Gemma again. *Nope. Where the heck did she go?* Violet sighed. *Okay, well, he's literally about to leave so he probably isn't a murderer. He could've done that already if he wanted.*

"Wait!" The word left her mouth before she'd fully okayed it. At this point, her arm was tired from holding this damn dress up and she just wanted to see it properly, so screw it.

He slowed and looked over his shoulder. "I thought the store was closed?" he teased.

"We are closed," she bit back, "but you did offer to help me, so..."

She waited as he turned and made his way to her. Assuming he would do the same, Violet made few attempts to hide her roaming eyes. Broad shoulders and strong arms filled out his wool jacket in a way that made her suspect his chest would be the coziest place one could possibly curl up. An unbuttoned Henley shirt gave way to wisps of chest hair that mimicked the same stunning salt and pepper color of his curls. She watched him flex his hand as he approached and imagined it gripping her tight enough to leave a few fingerprints. Everything about him was commanding, confident, and enticing.

When he stopped at the archway once more, her eyes shot up to his, only to find that he hadn't been brazenly checking her out at all. Instead, he studied her face with a grin that told her he'd caught every moment of her lack of subtlety.

Oops.

Well, if he'd needed his ego stroked, she'd certainly provided. Though something told her that was the last thing he needed. Her lips parted as she searched for something to say to dissipate the charged silence around her, but before she could speak, he motioned with his finger for her to turn around.

Violet dropped her arm to her side and presented her back to him. The satin of her dress drifted open, and she felt the heat of his hands as they hovered over her bare skin. His knuckles grazed her spine as he zipped up the dress in a moment that seemed to last a century. Then he stepped away and the warmth that his closeness provided faded.

She tried to compose herself, silently instructing her heartbeat to chill out. She avoided glancing back at him as she made her way to the mirror. *Damn.* She'd tried on countless evening gowns in her time working here, but this one took the cake. The slight cowl neck fell at just the right height to tease her cleavage. The zipper, finally closed, rested at the midpoint of her back, leaving her shoulders and plenty of skin bare. Every shift of her body had the silkiness of the fabric slipping across her skin.

"This might be the prettiest dress I've ever worn," she whispered to herself, forgetting another person was in the room at all.

Not on Mr. Sexy's watch. "You're breathtaking." He stepped into the reflection of the mirror, demanding her attention. "Definitely a keeper."

It took a minute for Violet to realize he was referring to the dress and not her. *Omg, get your head out of your ass, Vi.*

She scoffed quietly, but he either didn't notice or didn't care to comment. Sometimes she forgot the way that customers often assumed the employees here made enough to actually buy the merchandise.

Violet took another longing glance at the gown. The magic of the evening was waning now. Reality was clawing its way back in. She offered herself a small, encouraging smile in the mirror, then turned to square up to Mr. Sexy.

He leered at her, sensing her attitude had shifted. Again, she was all business.

"Well, I appreciate the help, but—"

"But we're closed. And I'll have to do my holiday shopping tomorrow," he mocked her remark from earlier.

She cocked an eyebrow at him.

"Here," he whispered, stepping closer. They were nearly chest to chest now, and Violet looked up at him in surprise through her lashes.

"What—" she began, but her breath caught in her throat as his hands snaked around her. His gaze focused on the mirror behind her where he could watch as his fingers grasped the zipper and tugged it down until the opening rested at the lowest point of her back. He released her and backed up, consistently ensuring that when he shared her space, it was fleeting, enough to taunt her, to leave her skin on fire and her tongue bitten to keep from gasping.

"Thank you," Violet murmured.

"You're most welcome."

Then he was gone, striding toward the exit again, and again she watched as he left. This time, he made it all the way out the door, never looking back.

Violet ran a hand through her hair in exasperation. *Okay. That's enough excitement for one night.*

* * *

Her shift the following day started in the early afternoon. Even with all day to get ready, Violet was still running late. She bustled through the back door of the department store and hurried down the short hall that led to the break room. The door smacked against the wall when she flung it open, startling the only other person in the room.

"Gemma, what the hell!"

Today, Violet's sweet, redheaded best friend sported two braids that hung down to her shoulders. Her wide, round glasses rested on the tip of her nose, and she was munching on something that had powdered sugar drifting down onto the table where she sat.

"Well, hello to you too, sunshine," Gemma's lilting voice rang with sarcasm.

"You totally abandoned me last night! Thanks to you, I got ambushed by Mr. Sexy and you didn't even get to see the dress of the century," Violet groaned as she shoved her purse and jacket in her locker.

"Hold on, who's Mr. Sexy?"

"Oh, wouldn't you like to know!"

Gemma giggled and stood up to brush powdered sugar off her shirt. "Why yes, yes, I would. I'm *sorry* I left last night. I got a call from my own Mr. Sexy with last minute dinner reservations that I would love to gush to you about, but you go first."

Violet crossed her arms and pouted at her friend. "Well... I don't actually know his name." She recounted the evening's events to her friend, complete with a few choice fantasies that hadn't happened but that she wouldn't have turned her nose up at.

"So, you're late because you spent all morning daydreaming about your Christmas mystery man?" Gemma concluded.

She shrugged. "More or less."

They were heading out to the sales floor now. Violet tugged on her stupid elf hat that the managers insisted everyone wear during the holidays because "we've got to play the part of Santa's little helpers!"

Gemma held the door wide for Violet but then clapped a hand on her friend's shoulder to pull her back. "Vi, wait." She nodded to a beautifully wrapped gift box on the table by the door. "That's got your name on it."

Violet picked up the box and examined the tag. *To: Violet Hawthorne* but the "from" signifier was blank. She glanced at Gemma.

"Omg, just open it! I'm not getting any younger over here."

Violet rolled her eyes. Carefully, she tugged at the golden bow and untaped the glittery, red wrapping paper. The box inside was just as pretty as the wrapping itself. The image of a tree decorated in red and green, standing in a field of snow and surrounded by other evergreens sprinkled with white stared back at her. She lifted the lid to peek inside.

"It's the dress," she gasped, tossing the lid aside for Gemma to see.

"Damn, that is gorgeous. Looks like you're someone's Ms. Sexy."

"Gemma, I can't accept this."

"Like hell you can't! Let yourself be spoiled, Vi. You deserve it." Gemma bumped her shoulder against Violet's gently. "*And you don't even know who to give it back to, remember?*"

Violet nodded absently. *Well, she's got me there.*

"Now, put that thing in your locker and come on before two little elves have to find new employment."

✳ ✳ ✳

Violet spent the first hour or two of her shift just going through the motions. Her mind drifted to memories of rough fingertips against her skin and the scent of smoke and bourbon filling her nostrils. It wasn't until a squeal pierced the air that she fell into the present.

Children were lining up to meet Santa for the first time of the season. Violet heard her and Gemma's names through her earpiece with instructions for them to be on crowd control. It took all her resolve to keep her head from dropping back in annoyance. Wrangling rambunctious kids was the last thing she wanted to do today.

She felt a pat on her back. "Deep breaths," Gemma chided in her ear. "Don't look so grumpy."

"Just call me Scrooge..."

Gemma's high-pitched laugh split the air. She roped her arm through Violet's and tugged her forward. "Come on."

Santa's desk was in one of the far corners of the store where the display team had constructed a whole office for him with makeshift walls and a fake fireplace. On the walls hung art of reindeer and Mrs. Claus, and atop the grand desk was a long list of names on parchment that rolled off the tabletop on either side and rested on the floor. Santa's desk chair featured a tall back wrapped in maroon leather with brass studs creating a lattice pattern from top to bottom. The fabricated scent of cinnamon and Christmas trees was almost overbearing.

Violet and Gemma herded children into a single file line as best they could while instructing parents to wait for their youngsters off to the side. Finally, "Santa Claus is Coming to Town" began drifting from the overhead speakers, signaling that the department store's hired Santa was on his way.

"Who's playing the part this year?" Violet whispered to Gemma. "Teddy again?"

"Nah, Teddy is spending like two months in Baltimore with his daughter and new grandbaby for the holidays."

"How dare he," Violet joked.

"I know, right? Like, where's my invite? Anyway, there's a new Santa this year. I think you'll like him, though. I heard he's super-hot. He's not even getting paid for this. He volunteered. Said it's his way of giving back. He made a big donation to the toy drive, too. His name is Santiago, but everyone keeps calling him Santi. Maybe he'll get your mind off Mr. Sexy." Gemma flashed a grin.

"Try telling him you're on the naughty list."

"Very funny." Still, hot Santa didn't sound half bad. She watched as the door in one of the fake walls swung open. Behind it, Violet knew, was the entrance to the back where the break room was, a place for Santas, Easter Bunnies, and other department store actors to prepare for seasonal events. A storewide announcement encouraged shoppers to clap and cheer for the "man with the beard." Then, adorned in possibly the nicest Santa suit Violet had ever seen, in walked Santiago.

The kids at her feet bounced and shoved to try and get a closer look. Cheers could be heard throughout the store, even by patrons too far away to see. *Santa* took to his desk and gazed out at the crowd, grinning. Then his eyes locked with Violet's in a way that left her feeling frozen in place.

Oh. My. God.

She contemplated the security of her job if she made a break for it. Or maybe she could simply melt into the floor and no one would notice? Anything to avoid the piercing eyes of the man she'd spent all night and day fantasizing about—her very own Mr. Sexy.

Every chance he got, he found her in the crowd. She ushered children to and fro for their chance to tell Santa what they wanted for Christmas, and he followed her every move, all the while playing his part effortlessly. When at last the final kids made their way back to their parents, Santi stood and waved before making his exit. Violet took the opportunity to hurry back to her regular post, and she almost made it, too. Then a hand closed around her wrist. *Damn it.*

"Not so fast, little elf." Had his voice somehow become *more* alluring since last night?

She turned to smile sweetly at him. He had traded his red suit for a cable knit sweater that stretched across his torso in a way that made her mouth water. She willed her embarrassment to present instead as sass.

"Violet," she corrected. "And you're Santiago, right? Or would you prefer Santa?"

"Santi, actually. Did I forget to mention that yesterday?"

"Among other things," she scolded.

"You're right." He began backing up but made no attempt to release her, guiding her instead behind Santa's office and toward the break room. "Allow me to make it up to you."

She let him lead her, albeit clumsily, as her eyes darted around to see if anyone noticed them.

"I—I can't accept it, Santi." She was sincere for a moment as she thought of the gown, knowing now that he had to be the one who had gifted it. Meanwhile she tried desperately to ignore how pleasant his name sounded on her lips.

"I don't think Santa has a return policy." He closed the door behind them and released her at last, but only to crowd in closer. "Besides, I want you to wear it when I take you out tonight." Santi placed his hands against the painted cinderblock wall on either side of her.

"Someone's presumptuous," she managed, though coherent thought wasn't exactly coming easy to her at the moment. It was all she could do to keep herself from leaning in and inhaling. The man was truly intoxicating.

Santi brushed the pad of his thumb over her bottom lip, freeing it from her teeth. She hadn't realized she'd been chewing it in the first place. "Well, I have a little holiday magic on my side, after all." He stepped closer until they were just a breath away and dropped his head to use the tip of his nose to trace a line from her collarbone to her jaw.

"Come on, Violet," Santi whispered. "Let me take out the most beautiful woman, in the prettiest dress she's ever worn, for a night of Christmas joy."

Joy. That had been at the top of her wish list, after all.

Reticent or not, she couldn't deny the magnetic hold he had on her. *One night with hot Santa? Why not?* She could already hear Gemma's voice in her mind telling her to go, have fun, *be naughty.* Finally, Violet nodded. "All right, but it better be one hell of an evening," she teased.

Santi grinned. His fingers gripped her chin just enough to hold her gaze on his. "That's my girl."

A small gasp escaped her but was just as quickly consumed as Santi's lips descended on her own. Their kiss was both passionate and fleeting. His tongue darted out for the briefest of moments before pulling away, despite her invitation for more. He had no intention of giving in to her just yet. Instead, Santi left Violet with a promise of more to come.

Do You Hear What I Hear?

Susan Dickenson

I can't believe I lost my locket," Jessica said to Michelle as she plopped down on a wooden stool at her best friend's breakfast bar. She perched her elbow on the counter, then cupped her chin in her hand. A long, exasperated sigh filled the room with her misery. "I thought being on my own for the first Christmas after 12 years of marriage was bad enough."

Knowing how much the locket meant to Jessica, Michelle's heart broke for her when she saw the sullen expression on her face. "Do you want to go back to the mall and look for it?"

Jessica sighed again and wiped a tendril of blonde hair away from her face. "I don't want to tie up your entire day. You have so much to do to get ready for your family's Christmas dinner."

Michelle poured a cup of hot tea. "Christmas is a week away, Jess. Here, try this."

Jessica righted herself, managed a slight smile, and took the mug. It warmed her cold hands as she breathed in the steam coming off the tea. "Hmm. That's an interesting aroma. Blackberry?"

"That's one of the ingredients," Michelle smiled. "It's called Heaven's Blend."

Jessica sipped the tea as she placed her left hand just below the hollow of her neck where her locket should have rested. She had not realized until it was gone just how many times a day she lovingly grasped it and rubbed her thumb over the pearl mounted in the center of the gold filigree locket.

Her Grandmother Jewell had told her to rub the pearl every once in a while to keep the pearl healthy and maintain its luster when she gifted the locket to Jessica. At first, she had to remind herself to rub the pearl as her grandmother had instructed, but eventually, it became a habit. She found it soothing to rub her thumb over the pearl's subtle imperfections. It felt almost like a map of her life, sometimes smooth, sometimes uneven, and in times of stress, she felt her grandmother's love and encouragement.

The separation from her husband was a devastating time. Not only did she lose her marriage just after Christmas that year, but her grandmother fell ill and passed quite suddenly. Jessica was mired in misery and felt life couldn't get much worse when her family home caught fire and was destroyed. All those generations of memories and trinkets were destroyed in a matter of minutes.

Jessica absentmindedly placed the mug on the kitchen counter, tears filling her eyes. "I wish heaven would help me find my locket. That's the only picture I have of my grandmother," she managed to say, forcing the words past the lump in her throat.

"That settles it. We're going back to the mall after we finish our tea," Michelle declared. She tilted her head, placing her hand on her hip. "And it might not hurt to ask for a little heavenly help."

* * *

Frustrated, Jessica stood staring at the mall's Nativity display as she absentmindedly listened to the Christmas carols playing over the sound system.

"Isn't it odd to believe that animals can speak on Christmas Eve?"

Jessica flinched. "What?"

"Oh, pardon me, I didn't mean to startle you," said an elderly man standing next to her. "Legend is that at midnight on Christmas Eve, animals can speak," he explained.

Jessica glanced at him quizzically. He had a kind face framed by wavy white hair, which in her opinion was a little too long for an elderly man, but it suited him somehow. He was dressed in quite the dapper plaid suit, all of which made him seem somewhat out of place for a busy mall. "I guess that's odd," she managed to reply.

He smiled and nodded toward the speaker in the ceiling. "A lamb speaks to a shepherd boy in the carol that's playing."

"I wasn't really listening," she admitted.

"You do seem a little lost—and alone," he noted.

"I'm sorry, do I know you?" Jessica asked.

"The name's Samuel."

"Well, Samuel, I'm not lost, but I did lose something. And I'm not alone," she stammered.

"When I lose something, I always retrace my steps, Jessica."

Exasperated, she turned back toward the Nativity. "I've been searching this mall all afternoon." Recalling the name of the carol, she said, "'Do You Hear What I Hear.'"

"What do you hear?" asked a different male voice.

Jessica looked to the spot where Samuel had stood but instead saw a handsome, although scruffy-bearded, brown-haired younger man smiling at her.

Embarrassed, she said, "That's the name of the carol playing over the sound system." She looked around for Samuel, but he was nowhere in sight.

"Waiting for someone?" he asked.

"There was an elderly gentleman standing here."

"The only person I saw as I walked up was you, Jess."

Jessica looked at the man again and felt her heart flutter as she recognized his shimmering blue eyes. "Kurt?"

He laughed at her expression. "I know, it's been a few years since high school."

"Try 15. I didn't recognize you," she said.

"You were a little preoccupied."

"I was standing here feeling sorry for myself when Samuel, the elderly man, began explaining about talking animals on Christmas Eve. He thought I looked lost, but I'm not lost; I lost something. Then I remembered the name of the carol, then you..."

"Whoa, slow down, Jess. I'm not sure who you were talking to, but like I said, you're the only person I saw standing here as I walked up from the food court."

"I don't understand. I know I didn't imagine him. He stood right here," she said, pointing at the spot where Samuel had been.

"Okay, okay," Kurt said, motioning his hands in a calming manner. "You said you lost something. What did you lose?"

"My locket. The pearl locket with Grandma Jewell's picture inside."

"I remember when your mom gave that to you," he said softly, placing his hand on her shoulder. "I'm so sorry I missed your grand-mother's funeral. I was stationed overseas and couldn't get home."

"I have wondered about you over the years," she admitted. "I'm sorry things ended so abruptly before you left for basic training. I'm not sure I even remember what happened."

"Life happened, Jess. We were young, just beginning our lives, and couldn't get on the same page. You don't have to apologize for anything," he assured her. "I'm home now, though," he said sheep-ishly. "Several years ago, my whole right side took some shrapnel from an IED. After I healed, I couldn't shoulder an M4 properly, let alone complete a standard recon, so they put me behind a desk. I never thought I'd retire at 33, but I applied for medical retirement. They approved it just a few months ago."

This time, it was her turn to comfort him. "Kurt, I had no idea," she said, placing her hand on his arm.

"I just see it as my next chapter," he grinned. "So, tell me what happened today," he said, changing the subject to the matter at hand.

Jessica smiled. *This is the Kurt I remember*, she thought. *Kind, considerate, and to the point.*

"I had my locket on this morning when Michelle and I went shopping, but I noticed I didn't have it on as I got out of the car at her house," she explained. "We looked all through her car and in our shopping bags, but it was nowhere to be found."

"Have you tried retracing your steps?" he asked.

"That's exactly what Samuel suggested," she sighed. "I have been all over this mall." Jessica glanced around. "Michelle is somewhere around here looking, too."

"I'm sorry. I know how much it means to you, Jess."

"Fifteen years later and you still know how to make me feel better." *Why did I ever let him go?* she thought.

"What did Samuel say about talking animals?" Kurt asked abruptly.

"He said that on Christmas Eve, animals can speak," she replied.

A perplexed expression creased his brow. "And what animal speaks in that Christmas carol?" he asked.

Frowning, she replied, "A lamb?"

"Jess, do you see what I see?" Kurt asked as he stared at the Nativity.

Jessica followed the direction of Kurt's gaze. There, hanging on the lamb's neck, was her locket. "How on earth did it get there?" she wondered.

Kurt carefully climbed over the velvet rope surrounding the Nativity. He stared at the lamb for a moment before he reached down to open the clasp of the necklace to retrieve it. After righting himself with an all-too-familiar groan, he crossed back over the rope, walked back to Jessica, and placed it around her neck.

"Samuel called me Jessica," she whispered as she touched the pearl on the face of her locket. "I never told him my name."

"It is the season of miracles, Jess."

She smiled, placing her hand on Kurt's scruffy cheek. "I received two miracles today. Maybe it's time for me to start my next chapter."

"I wouldn't mind helping you write it, if you wouldn't mind helping me write mine," he offered.

"Deal," she said as she gently grasped his hand. "Now, let's find Michelle. She makes the best tea!"

* * *

Sitting at a little café table on the other side of the mall's court-yard, an elderly man dressed in a dapper plaid suit with a kind face framed by wavy white hair, a little too long for an elderly man, smiled and sipped a cup of steaming tea.

"Hmm, Heaven's Blend," he said. "What a beautiful day for a good cup of tea and a Christmas miracle."

I Want to Go Home

Linda Hudson Hoagland

Standing under the leafless limbs of the maple tree, I try to hide from the sight of the helicopter flying overhead. It's almost Christmas, so why are they out today?

I do not want to be found. I want to go home. Why can't I go home?

"What's the point of running away if someone finds you?" I whisper as I peek from beneath the limbs.

I step forward to gauge the "whop-whop" sounds echoing through the valley from the flying eggbeater.

Hopefully, that whirling contraption is running a hospital shuttle and not looking for me. That's what it is. They are transporting a seriously ill patient from the local hospital to a facility with the doctors and machines it takes to keep that patient alive.

They wouldn't be looking for me. I'm just a crazy old lady out taking a walk the day before Christmas because no one has come to visit me. The place is buzzing with visitors, but none of them are mine. It doesn't matter to anyone that I'm traveling away from my familiar surroundings in this place they want me to call home, not towards my safe harbor of home and hearth.

I guess I'm living up to the label of crazy old lady because I keep talking to myself. People don't realize you have to talk to yourself so you can hear a human voice, even if it is only your own voice that flows through the air.

I am walking and walking to an unknown destination. It doesn't matter to me about where I am going. It only matters that I am going, because…

"Why am I running away?" I ask loudly.

When I get no response, I stop walking.

"Why am I running away?" I ask again. "Where am I going?"

The tears start sliding down my cheeks. I've done it again. I don't know where I am or how I got here. I can't remember why I'm running away or where I am going. My mind keeps telling me I have to leave. Leave where?

All I want to do is go home.

"Please God, help me go home," I pleaded.

"Where is home?" I say as I spin round and round and round, until I fall to the ground motionless and barely breathing.

My eyes are open, and I am staring up into the sky. I am not moving. I feel my slow, shallow breaths making my chest slightly move with the effort.

I force myself up from where I had been resting on the light skiff of snow-covered ground. I tug at my thin sweater, pulling the sides to the front so I can button it.

"I'm so cold," I say as I cross my arms with my hands touching my elbows, protecting myself from the little bit of wind that has started to stir the tall spikes of browned grass, sifting the snow to the ground.

I'm not wearing a jacket or coat to protect me from Mother Nature's onslaught of winter. It is winter, isn't it?

"It's snowing!" I shout as I dance around, extending my arms and manipulating my hands to catch a flake. Snow makes me so happy. I haven't seen snow since—I can't remember when.

"Why can't I remember when?" I ask as I plop down on my behind, hitting my backside so hard that it jars my teeth.

The ground is cold against my bottom, so I straighten my legs out, roll over, getting closer to a tree so I can use the tree to balance myself as I push myself to get to my knees, then I pull myself up from my knees using the trunk of the tree to assist me. It is not a pretty sight, but it's the best I can do.

I'm standing upright now, looking around, focusing on my surroundings.

"Why am I here?" I mumble as I try to figure out in which direction I should walk.

I look at my feet and discover that I have on house slippers. I'm not wearing real shoes. I look at my legs and see that I am dressed in pajamas, not clothes.

"Where are my clothes? Someone stole my clothes," I whisper conspiratorially.

I propel myself forward, windmilling my arms, trying to move faster towards a paved area. I couldn't tell if it was a sidewalk or a street. It would be so much easier to walk on pavement than on this uneven ground.

I trudge ahead, moving toward the pavement when I spot movement off to my right side. It was so quick—the movement, I mean—that I couldn't determine if it was man or beast.

Should I speed up or stop and confront the spectacle that is trying to frighten me?

I slow my pace a little so I can get a better look. I gaze at the cluster of bushes searching for what caused the movement.

"It was only the wind," I whisper with a sigh of relief.

Farther, I move toward the pavement up ahead. I'm not moving very fast, but I am old, and rapid movement is not in my future anymore. I haven't seen anyone outside, so no one must be missing me. I must live alone. No one even cares that I'm gone.

My mind flashes back to a family. Two young boys and a man are at the center of the memory flash. I recognize the man as Sammy, my husband, and the two boys are Eddy and Aaron, my two sons.

"Where are they? Why aren't they here to see me? To help me? To take me back to my home? Where is my home?" I ask as I spin around, looking for a familiar sight.

"Ellen, don't move. Stay right there!" screams a voice as I am about to set my foot onto the pavement.

"What do you want?" I shout back as loud as I can, but I know the screamer didn't hear me.

"Don't move, Ellen! Please don't move!" an angry voice yells at me. At least, he sounds angry to me.

"Why?" I ask as I feel my anger rise and warm my cold body.

Suddenly, out of nowhere, a male form springs at me and grabs me from behind. I struggle against his muscular arms that have my arms pinned down to my sides.

"Let go of me! I want to go home," I sputter as I struggle to free myself of the vice-grip arms.

"Settle down, Ellen, I can't let you go. You will fall into the water if I let you go."

"What water?"

"Right in front of you. The pond is right there. Don't you see it? You have to go around the pond to get to the road."

"I was trying to get to the road so it wouldn't be so hard to walk. I seem to have my house slippers on my feet for some reason. Why am I dressed in my pajamas? Who are you?" I say in a makeshift explanation, followed by questions for which I truly need answers.

"I'm going to pull you back away from the water. Do you understand what I'm saying?" asks the man dressed in white.

"Yes, I understand."

He pulls me away from the water in an awkward position because he won't release his arms from the grip on my body. We sort of scoot back one small step at a time.

When he feels it is safe, he finally loosens his grip.

"You aren't going to run, are you, Ellen?"

"No, not if you tell me who you are."

"I'm Jerry; I work here at this facility. It is my job to keep you safe and out of harm's way. How did you get out here? You know you aren't supposed to go walking alone," he says in a scolding tone.

I turn so I can see his face. It looks familiar, but I really can't place it.

"Where is Sammy? Why aren't my sons here?" I ask as I try to hold back the rush of tears that I can feel rolling down my cheeks.

"Your son Eddy will be here this weekend. Aaron can't visit right now because he lives too far away. He will call this weekend. You told your sons to put you here to keep you safe, because you have Alzheimer's. Sammy passed away, Ellen. He can't visit you anymore. Do you remember now?"

"I'm so cold," is all I can say.

He leads me away, holding onto my hand so I can't possibly sneak out of his sight. He takes me to my room, removes my slippers, and tells me to get into bed as he pulls the covers up to my chin so I can get warm.

"I wish I could go home. I know I get confused, but I will never forget how much I love Sammy and my boys," I whisper before falling asleep.

Magic

April Hensley

As the soloist sang the last verse of "Silent Night," the portrait of Jesus seemed to glow, illuminated by hundreds of tiny flickering candle flames. Garlands and wreaths made of real greenery and topped with red velvet bows decorated every pew and window, adding a stout, fresh pine scent to the faint aroma of melted wax. A brightly decorated tree filled the front corner at the left of the sanctuary. When the last haunting strains of the song reverberated through the sanctuary, not another sound could be heard. After the last note faded, thunderous applause filled the space.

Ava Wilson turned to her left and warmly hugged fair-haired Beth Johnson. The Wilson Christmas Eve celebration had run late, and the young wife and mother had to rush to the church to make it on time. Beth had saved Ava a seat near the front. Best friends since kindergarten, they chatted about tomorrow's holiday plans as they tugged on their coats, Ava proudly adjusting her new, red, plaid scarf under her long, glossy, ebony hair. The scarf and a pair of matching gloves had been a gift from her sweet mother-in-law.

Ava stepped out of the pew into the tight herd of people steadily heading for the door. As they slowly made their way out, fellow parishioners were calling to each other with heartfelt Christmas wishes and greetings. Ava and Beth smiled and chatted with so many people, shaking hands and sharing hugs.

There had been a magical feeling in the air that Christmas Eve. Warm conversation and rich laughter had flowed at Ava's husband Gabriel's family celebration. At the late church service, the powerful spiritual message of the Nativity stirred Ava's soul to childlike wonder. It brought home to Ava how even the Son of God had a humble start during his time on earth.

Magic was just what Ava needed in a year that had not been so great. As Ava looked around, she could see a strained expression on a few faces, even though it had been almost a year since the plant closure. The company had been the Southwest Virginia town's biggest employer. Everyone in Cedar Valley had been affected in some way, including her little family. She hadn't felt much magic this year. But today, it felt like magic was all around her.

Pastor Jenkins stood at one of the doors leading into the foyer. He took Ava's hand lightly and wished her a heartfelt thank you for coming. He was a new pastor, young and unmarried but passionate about his calling, with a calm and lighthearted personality. His eyes seemed to mirror an old soul. The theme of the night had been the Nativity, but he also spoke about the legend of the animals talking at midnight on Christmas Eve. The pastor mused, "I wonder what the animals would have said to Mary and Joseph in the stable." Ava, being an animal lover, was thrilled to hear of the old story.

Ava left the church close to midnight and stepped reverently into the crisp winter air. It had started to snow sometime in the last hour. It was as if she were stepping into a mini snow globe.

The flakes moved like sparkling glitter dancers, falling gracefully and then swooping up and away, never reaching the ground over the parking lot. Adults awed with wonder while sleepy children ran around trying to catch snowflakes on their tongues.

It had been an especially mild winter so far. Even though it was snowing, the temperature was still fair with no biting wind. Their home garden even had a couple of straggling plants that insisted on trying to produce a few more cherry tomatoes. After tonight's freeze, those would be gone too. The garden would finally get a well-deserved rest until spring.

The service had been enchanting and humbling, the feeling carrying right out into the parking lot. The midnight start time had been changed to 10 p.m. this year since most of the congregation wanted to get up early on Christmas morning. Calling out her last holiday best wishes, Ava hugged her bestie and headed to her small hatchback.

The church was on the outskirts of town. Ava had rarely driven this road at night. Leaving the parking lot, she turned right back towards town. It was a short 10-minute drive home. Gabriel and the twins had been going to come to the service too, but the four-year-olds had been exhausted from an evening of playing with their young cousins. Gabe had offered to take them home. Ava had a sneaking suspicion that her husband was trying to get a surprise present finished for her, too. Also, he knew she wanted—and needed—to go to church. She had leaned heavily on her faith this year.

Dark pines lined both sides of the road. Ava watched the road carefully, not needing the deer crossing sign to be alert. Not far after carefully going through a curve, three deer stood to the side of the road. Usually, they would dart away when a car approached. Appearing to have no fear of her, they made eye contact with Ava through the windshield. Their beautiful, gentle brown eyes were rimmed with thick lashes. All females. The one in the front followed Ava's path with its head turning, watching as she crawled slowly past, mesmerized by their beauty.

Ava's mind drifted as she made her way home. She had woken up with a feeling of dread this morning, though it was no different than any other morning since New Year's Day. Gabe had been one of the ones who lost their job when the plant closed. She'd prayed again for God to watch over them. It felt like the dark cloud had lifted more and more as the day went on.

She had barely had time to dwell on her worries this morning when she was greeted excitedly by the twins. Benjamin and Breanna jumped on the bed, hugging their mother, excited to have both their parents at home. Within moments, Otis, their giant, charcoal gray and silver Alaskan Malamute, and Tabitha, a sassy, black, oversized cat, joined them on the bed. Appearing suddenly, burly Gabriel launched himself from the door onto the bed, causing everyone to bounce and dissolving the whole crew into fits of laughter, barking, and giggling.

Gabe had already been in the kitchen, whipping up breakfast. He had grabbed his wife around the waist, pulling her in for a loving kiss. They didn't get to see each other much, so today had been a real treat.

After breakfast, Ava cleaned up while Gabe went out to the garage to finish up some Christmas presents for his family. Ava had decided to bake bread and make candy as gifts. The twins were now old enough that they were fun helpers in the kitchen, if a little messy, too. Otis and Tabitha hung out, waiting for mistakes to land on the floor.

Things had been tight this year. Ava and Gabe had had a perfect life in their cute little bungalow, a gentle stream flowing on the edge of the backyard with their spunky twins and their beloved pets. They weren't well off by any means, but they had what they needed. Then, out of nowhere, with no notice, the plant had closed down on New Year's Day.

Gabe was made of sterner stuff, though. He might have been as shocked as everyone else, but he didn't let it keep him down. Ava's husband was an avid fisherman and started making fishing baits. The business had taken off quickly, but they had gone through all their savings to get it going. The profit wasn't what he'd been making when he had worked at the factory, but it looked like, with the growth, in two years, they would be back where they had been. Who knew after that? Like Gabe said, people were never going to stop fishing, no matter what happened with the economy.

Plus, saving the cost of daycare was a bonus. The kids stayed home with Gabe while he worked during the day out of the garage. Ava worked at the optometrist's office, managing the front desk. Her employer had given her plenty of overtime hours every week to help, but she missed getting to spend time with Gabe and her two-legged and furry kids, and just getting to be a wife and mom.

Sometimes Ava lay awake at night trying to think of ways to tell Gabe she wanted him to find a regular job, one that was a guaranteed income. But when the anxious young woman woke up every morning and saw her husband's excited face, she kept the fears and worries to herself. Sometimes Ava thought he could see the worry in her eyes and would hug her gently. Gabe would whisper, "Don't worry, darling. I've got this. We are going to be okay. You don't need to work so much."

She felt like she'd been holding her breath for 12 months waiting on disaster to strike again. Every day, his great mood would build her through the whole day, but she spent the nights praying for God to help them through.

A few blocks before she reached home, Ava slowed at a small, shadowy movement on the edge of the road. At first, she thought it was a dog but quickly realized by the tall, big ears and long nose that it was a red fox. Just as the deer had done, it sat motionless, watching her as if beckoning her closer. Ava rolled her window down to get a better look. Its big, deep brown eyes glowed in the dim light of the streetlamp. With a blink, it disappeared into the woods bordering the road, making Ava wonder if she'd really seen it after all.

As Ava pulled into their driveway a short distance away, the snowflakes got bigger and stickier. She sat in the car outside the garage quietly thinking of a year that was almost over, feeling relaxed and content.

The garage was no longer used to park their cars. It was filled with tables covered in molds and a rainbow of different-colored, soft, plastic worms and bugs waiting to be packaged and shipped. Even though Ava had been afraid of all the unexpected changes, she felt a deep pride in Gabe for working so hard to make a future for them.

The homemade baked gifts had been a huge hit, much to Ava's surprise. Everybody had gotten fishing baits, even the ones who didn't fish, including Gabe's 84-year-old grandmother, which caused a lot of laughter. Gabe had made wooden pull toys for all the nieces and nephews. Ava hadn't missed the craziness and expense of shopping for presents, but she wanted to give gifts to family so they would feel loved. She had felt some hesitation but didn't want to go empty-handed. Now she knew they would probably do homemade and handmade gifts from now on.

Suddenly, a big, furry head popped out of the pet door in the side of the garage. With a big grin, Otis looked over at Ava still sitting in the car. They had installed a pet door in the garage so he could come and go to the fenced backyard when he chose. In the winter, he was more outside than inside.

As soon as Ava stepped from the car, the fluffy dog ran to the gate to greet her excitedly. With wolflike color and markings, Otis could be mistaken for a predator, but that thought wouldn't last long. His tail was always wagging, and his mouth opened in a happy smile. He loved people. It would appear he would make a bad guard dog, but he loved his family. At over a hundred pounds, luckily, it had never had to be tested.

Ava and Otis went way back, before even Gabe. Otis had been a real trooper as their little family grew. Once, it had just been the two of them, and they had depended on each other. Ava tried not to notice how he was getting a little grayer around his muzzle. He and Gabe had loved each other from their first meeting. Half the time, he treated the twins as if he were their babysitter and the other half as a playful big brother.

Ava went straight to the backyard to spend time with him. She would have loved for him to be a house dog, but Otis would only come inside during thunderstorms or to sleep in front of the air conditioner in the sizzling summer heat. He loved winter. The temperatures were perfect for him with his thick coat suited for snowier climates than Southern Virginia.

Ava crouched down in front of Otis, and he sat facing her. Otis's big brown eyes were not unlike the deer and the fox.

She ran her fingers over his face and through his fur, all the while asking about his night and if he liked his new big bone that "Santa" had given him earlier for Christmas. He quivered with excitement and contained energy. Otis's gentle eyes stared deeply into

Ava's as she talked to him. Tiny crystal snowflakes stuck to his dense hair. The dawn-to-dusk light shining down on them made him look like he was covered in a million miniature stars.

It was then that Ava again remembered the pastor talking about animals being able to speak on Christmas Eve at midnight. *Oh no,* she thought. Maybe she'd already missed midnight, but a quick look at her watch showed her it was a few seconds before. She bent closer to Otis, and he leaned closer to her. As she asked him quietly if he was going to talk to her, his eyes widened, his ears perked up, and he wiggled closer to her again. It felt like time stood still. She was holding her breath. His usual smiling face was serious as his eyes were locked onto Ava's. There was age-old wisdom in his eyes.

Quickly, he moved. Instantly, the spell was broken by a big wet swipe of his tongue up Ava's cheek. She alternated between laughing and saying yuck while wiping off the sticky, slobbery kiss. Otis sat calmly watching, back to normal with his usual wide grin.

She gave him a big, loving hug before getting up to head towards the house. He walked beside her on the way to the door until a small, brown bunny huddled in the shadows caught his eye. He took off on his futile nightly chase.

Ava could see Tabitha, their black, oversized housecat, waiting patiently inside the full-view sliding patio door. Tabitha threw her paw up on the glass like she was waving at Ava. She could also see Gabe wrestling a big roll of wrapping paper at the kitchen table. She couldn't wait to snuggle with her sweet fur babies and Gabe on the couch in front of the fireplace.

Ava would have loved to have heard Otis or Tabitha speak to her on this beautiful, holy night. They already talked to her and the whole family every day, though. They communicated with their hearts, more than any spoken words could ever say.

Unexpectedly, it came to her what she'd been feeling all day. It was not magic, yet it was magic. It was the magic of a special, precious gift Ava felt so blessed to give and get in return—spending time with the people and souls she loved. She hadn't spent much time with anyone, including her pets and children, in the past year. She had been terrified of losing their home and going without. Ava had given up her loved ones to make more money until there was no magic left in her life.

Ava had prayed to God to help them get through. She finally realized that He did. The young woman had just been too busy to notice.

Yes, it had been a very magical Christmas Eve because Ava was surrounded by the best gift of all. It was love.

The Man in the Red Suit

Jan Howery

With her coat tucked under her arm, Mary Jane walked outside and looked up at the sky. The fast-moving clouds swirled around the moon, creating a full halo. *Ma always said that was a promise of bad weather looming,* she thought as she walked through the parking lot to her car.

Mary Jane, a nurse practitioner, worked the emergency admittance on nightshift at the Bethlehem Hospital. Her shift was the 3:00 p.m. to 11:00 p.m., and tomorrow she would be working a double shift. She volunteered to work because it was Christmas Eve. She didn't mind working on holidays so others could spend the holiday with their families. She was divorced and lived alone, except for her cat, Donut. She lived near the hospital in a patio home community which was across the highway from the hospital, and it was easy to walk to work. Tonight, she didn't walk to work because she planned to go by the grocery store to pick up some last-minute items since the weather forecast predicted a big snowstorm arriving on Christmas Eve.

After her shopping, she got home around 1:00 a.m. She greeted Donut with a treat, settled back in her favorite chair, sipped on a glass of red wine, and stared into the low burning flames of the fireplace. "It's going to be just you and me this Christmas," she said out loud. Donut purred as if in understanding.

Mary Jane looked at her beautifully decorated Christmas tree and felt sad to be alone. Her parents passed away a few years ago, just a few months apart from the pandemic, and she had no siblings. Shortly after their passing, she found comfort when someone dropped off a small kitten at her doorstep on Christmas morning in a crumbled, sweet-smelling donut box. That was how Donut got her name. "I guess someone knew I needed some companionship, and I have you," Mary Jane said. Again, Donut purred as if she understood.

The next day, Mary Jane loaded her car with gifts that she had bought for the children who wouldn't be leaving the hospital for the Christmas holiday. The staff chose names of the children patients and bought gifts from Santa Claus to hand out to the children. Santa Claus's arrival was scheduled for seven o'clock on Christmas Eve, as well as the arrival of the Christmas carolers, and a piano player playing favorite holiday tunes. With the food and drink provided, it would be a special Christmas Eve celebration.

Mary Jane arrived at the hospital at 2:30 p.m. and carried her gifts into the hospital cafeteria. "Look at all these gifts," a co-worker said.

"And don't they look beautiful under our gigantic Christmas tree?" Mary Jane asked as she placed her last group of presents under the tree. Suddenly, someone yelled, "Hey, look! It's starting to snow."

She looked out the window and said, "Let's hope Santa and his reindeer show up." Everyone giggled and agreed.

By six o'clock, the snow was falling steadily and parents were arriving for the anticipation of Santa's arrival. Mary Jane watched the clock. With each passing minute, she became more anxious. *Where is Santa Claus?* she thought. *It's almost seven.*

Mary Jane's cell phone beeped with a text message. It was from the receptionist at the front entrance.

There is a man here in a red suit. He is lost. Help?

Mary Jane quickly texted, **OTW.**

Mary Jane was surprised when she saw a handsome young man standing in the waiting room in a Santa suit holding a wig, beard, a red hat, and a big pillow. He looked around the room and appeared confused.

"You're not Mr. Davidson," Mary Jane said abruptly without saying hello.

"Yes, ma'am, I am. But my dad, Tom Davidson, got double-booked here and at the Alzheimer's wing, and I'm here to fill in for him. My name is Joe. I just need to go to a bathroom and finish dressing," Joe said. "I'm not too late, am I?"

Mary Jane smiled. "No, you're right on time. The bathroom is over to your right, and when you come out, follow me. I'm just glad that Santa showed up…be it the dad or the son."

When Joe came out of the bathroom, he fit the description of Santa Claus. The big pillow fit his tummy, and the wig and beard looked very authentic. The hat fit perfectly.

Mary Jane smiled and shook her head. "Quite the transformation!"

"HO, HO, HO, here I go," Joe laughed and winked.

Mary Jane escorted him to his throne-type chair that was placed in front of the Christmas tree, and everyone applauded as he got comfortable in the chair.

The evening was lively with Santa handing out gifts and the carolers singing and everyone taking pictures. By nine o'clock, it was time for the children to be taken back to their rooms, and the celebration was coming to an end.

"You did a wonderful job with all the kids, and the parents, too," Mary Jane whispered in Santa's ear. He stood and waved good-bye to all of them.

"HO, HO, HO to all, and have a very merry Christmas!" Santa yelled as he exited the room. Everyone applauded again.

Mary Jane followed Joe to the front entrance. "Thank you," she said and smiled. "That snow is really coming down. Will you be okay? I'm sure Mrs. Claus will be worried."

Joe hesitated and replied, "I'll be fine. My reindeer is a four-wheel drive…and there's no Mrs. Claus. Just Dad and me. Mom passed away a few years ago and I'm divorced. You? How did you get so lucky to be working on Christmas Eve?"

"I actually volunteered. My parents passed away during the pandemic and it's just me and my cat," Mary Jane shared. The conversation was interrupted when Mary Jane's phone beeped with a text.

The text read, **INCOMING**.

Joe noticed the change in Mary Jane's facial expression and looked over at her name tag. "Mary Jane…Guess that means you're needed somewhere. Just want you to know it was a pleasure meeting you, and I'm glad I could help out this evening."

"Yes. And thank you, again," Mary Jane said, turned, and walked toward the personnel-only emergency entrance. With a slight hand wave and smile, Joe walked out the front doors and headed out into the parking lot.

* * *

"There's been a bad crash on the interstate...Got four vehicles involved with injuries," one of the paramedics announced as they rushed in with the first patient. "Prepare for the worst. Roads are treacherous and no one should be out on the roads tonight. It's really snowing hard."

"Who's our first patient?" Mary Jane asked.

"He was pinned in his vehicle, trapped under a jackknifed tractor-trailer. We've tried to contact his next of kin listed in his phone contacts," the paramedic said.

Mary Jane gasped. "He's in a Santa suit," she said. "I know him. Let's get him back here quickly for evaluation."

"He's lucky to be alive. When his vehicle slid under the trailer, something caused his seatbelt to break loose, and he dropped over into the passenger seat...Otherwise, he would've probably been killed instantly," the paramedic said.

"Well...it is the night for miracles," Mary Jane said calmly.

* * *

Joe was almost to his truck when he became startled by the loud sirens of two ambulances rushing toward the emergency entrance. He hopped inside his truck and slowly removed his fake white beard, wig, hat, and wiggled to remove the pillow from his tummy. Snow covered his truck's windshield, and he started to get out of his truck to clear the window when his phone beeped. He had a voice message.

He listened.

"This is Officer Wiseman. I am trying to reach Joseph Davidson. There was a car crash involving a tractor-trailer on the interstate, and one of the injured has this name and number in his cell phone as the emergency contact for Thomas Davidson. I am sorry to leave this message, but Mr. Davidson was involved in this crash and has been taken to the Bethlehem Hospital. If possible, please go directly to the hospital or return this phone call."

"No! That's Dad!" Joe said and jumped out of his truck and rushed through the emergency room entrance to the check-in counter. "I need to speak to Mary Jane. Please page her. I need to speak with her ASAP. Now!"

"Please calm down, sir. I'll get her," the receptionist said.

Mary Jane's phone beeped with a text message.

There's a man in the waiting room wanting to speak with 'Mary Jane.' He insists. He's in a red suit.

Mary Jane texted, **OTW.**

The doctor entered the evaluation room. Mary Jane said, "This is Tom Davidson. He has superficial abrasions on his forehead and cheek. There is a persistent trickle of blood from a laceration at his scalp's right temple. The patient's right arm is limp. I gently palpated the limb, noting swelling and deformity at the forearm—classic signs of a possible fracture. The patient did groan, indicating consciousness. But there is possible internal bleeding."

"I'll take over here. You're needed out front," the doctor instructed.

Mary Jane walked to the exit doors, pushed the button, and the doors opened. She walked into the waiting area and looked around the waiting room. *A man in a red suit,* she thought. She was glancing around the room when she heard someone say, "Mary Jane."

She turned and faced the man in the red suit. It was a Santa Claus suit. "Joe?"

"Yes. Dad's been in a car accident. Have you seen him? Do you know…if…is he okay?" Joe asked in a panic. "Is he back there?"

"Calm down, Joe. He is being evaluated. He has a fractured arm, which will require surgery. I drew blood for lab tests, and he is being prepared for X-rays of the injured arm and a CT scan to rule out head or internal injuries. We are imaging for abdominal injuries as well. Your dad is alert, and the attending physician ordered intravenous fluids and IV analgesia. I will tell you more as I know, okay? Okay?" she said.

"Yes. Thank you. Can I see him…just to let him know that I'm here?" Joe asked.

"Not yet. But soon, okay?" Mary Jane said. "I will let him know that you're here."

Joe took a deep breath and replied, "Okay. I am concerned."

"Yes. I do understand. I will get back as soon as I know something. I'll see if you can come back and sit with him," Mary Jane said slowly and warmly.

Joe stared at Mary Jane and answered, "Okay. Do you think he's going to be okay?"

Mary Jane looked into Joe's big dark eyes. He had tears in them. Mary Jane grabbed Joe's hand and gave it a squeeze. Joe stepped forward and gave her a hug. Surprised, she stepped back and looked at him. She felt an instant familiarity. They stared at each other. The moment between them should have been awkward, but it wasn't.

"Yes. He's going to be okay," Mary Jane assured him.

"I'll get my change of clothes from the truck and be right back," Joe said.

Mary Jane nodded and turned quickly to walk back to Mr. Davidson's evaluation room. She asked the doctor, "When can the patient's son come back here and sit with him?"

The doctor darted a look in her direction and said, "After surgery. He can come back when the patient's out of surgery. And the patient's going into surgery now."

Mary Jane attended to the other crash victims. There were no fatalities, and as the paramedics brought in the last crash victim, one said, "The interstate's shut down. Roads are just impassable."

It was almost 3:00 a.m. when Mr. Davidson was assigned a patient's room. Mary Jane stepped out and found Joe slumped in a chair. His wavy, curly black hair fell gently onto his face. *He's very good looking,* Mary Jane thought.

"Joe," Mary Jane said quietly. "Joe, wake up."

"Yes," Joe stammered. "How's Dad?"

"He's out of surgery and doing fine," Mary Jane said. "His room number is 31225. Third floor, room 1225. He has no internal injuries."

"Thank God, and thank you," Joe said.

"Take the elevator around the corner, and I'll see you in his room," Mary Jane said.

Joe walked into the room and found his dad resting.

"Dad, can you hear me?" Joe asked.

"Joe?" his dad asked sleepily.

"Yes, Dad. It's me," Joe said. "You okay?"

His dad drifted back to sleep with a low, "Yeah."

Mary Jane walked into the room. "Joe, he's so sedated, he probably won't remember you being here. He's going to be okay. It's miracle that he survived, and with no serious injuries."

"Do you believe in miracles?" Joe asked and watched Mary Jane's reaction to his question.

Mary Jane smiled and answered, "Sure do."

Joe's dad's groans interrupted the conversation.

"I will check back in a few hours," Mary Jane said. "I can give you my phone number and you can text me if you need anything."

Joe quickly said, "Yes. That would be great. Thank you."

They exchanged phone numbers.

As Mary Jane's work shift ended at 7:00 a.m., she put on her coat and boots and grabbed her tote bag from her locker. She hurried to Mr. Davidson's room. Joe was resting in the recliner.

"Figured you might be asleep," Mary Jane said softly.

"No. Can't sleep. Dad seems to be resting, though. I would like to have a hot shower and shave. Guess I'll head home for a few hours' sleep and then come back. Don't tell me you're headed home. Are you going to drive on these roads?" Joe said.

Mary Jane giggled. "Yes, I am headed home…but I live over there." She pointed out the window toward the community, Manger's Way, located across the road.

"You live over there? That's convenient," Joe said. "But…don't you think that you…you might need someone to walk you home?"

Mary Jane blushed and asked, "Are you offering to walk me home?"

Joe blushed and smiled. "Yes. May I walk you home?"

They both laughed.

"Yes. You may walk me home," Mary Jane said.

Joe and Mary Jane pushed through the deep snow. The snow was still gently falling, and accumulation exceeded over a foot. They laughed and talked and acted like kids playing in the snow.

They crossed the highway and walked into the gated community.

Mary Jane said, "Not much farther. First right, Barnwell Street.

It's the last house on the right."

Joe took her hand, and they walked through the deep snow up slight incline. Without warning, Mary Jane's foot got stuck in the snow, and when she tried to step, she fell forward. Joe grabbed her waist and pulled her only to find himself falling backward into the snow.

They tumbled, and Mary Jane found herself laying on top of Joe. They both were laughing uncontrollably until their eyes met. They were drawn to each other. The magic of the moment sent shivers up Joe's spine.

Mary Jane tried to move. "I'm so sorry..."

"No. Don't apologize," Joe said seriously. He touched her face.

Mary Jane pulled away and rolled over into the snow. "We look like snowmen," Mary Jane said, trying to change the mood and the moment.

"Guess we do," Joe said, "but I do love the snow."

When they arrived at the front door of her house, Mary Jane turned to look at Joe and said, "Don't think that I am being forward here, but would you like to come in? I have a guest bedroom, and you can shower and rest here instead of driving on these bad roads."

Joe hesitated. "Are you okay with that?"

Mary Jane didn't answer. She unlocked the front door and walked inside, leaving Joe standing on the porch. She turned and said, "Yes, as long as you like cats."

"Well, it just so happens, I love cats." Joe walked inside and said, "Wow, what a nice place."

"Thank you. Down the hall, the guest bedroom is on the left, and make yourself comfortable. I'm going to shower and get some sleep. I'll get up about one o'clock. You can stay as long as you want," Mary Jane said.

Mary Jane showered and felt so confused. She hadn't experienced real emotions in such a long time that it puzzled her to find herself being attracted to a total stranger. She liked Joe. She wanted to be with Joe. She drifted off to sleep, thinking about his touch.

* * *

Mary Jane awoke when her alarm buzzed at 1:00 p.m. She got dressed and made her way to the kitchen to find Joe there, frying eggs.

"Good morning...or should I say good afternoon," Joe said enthusiastically. "I made myself at home in your kitchen. I found eggs, and I thought an egg sandwich sounded good."

"Sounds good to me, too," Mary Jane agreed and sat on the stool at the bar.

Joe toasted the bread, prepared the sandwiches, and put them on a plate and set them on the counter.

Mary Jane and Joe exchanged another long stare. She broke the silence by asking, "Do you believe in miracles?"

Joe smiled and said, "Yes. Do you believe in love at first sight?"

Mary Jane took a deep breath. "No..."

Joe looked down, appearing disappointed.

"...not until now," Mary Jane finished.

Donut purred in agreement.

The Christmas Wave

Kathleen M. Jacobs

for matt

...this our island in the wave...
— CHARLES DICKENS

As Christmas inched its way into Ginny Johnstone's life, knowing that once again she would spend Christmas Eve and Christmas Day alone, she stomped her feet that were snug inside her chestnut-colored UGG sheepskin slippers. The snow fell lightly outside her apartment window, which overlooked a triangular-shaped green space filled with overly decorated Fraser firs representing the city's businesses: a bookstore, a bakery, a pizzeria, a jewelry store, and quite a few breweries.

She wrapped her arms around herself in an effort to quell a chill that couldn't be warmed. The fierce wind threatened to topple each tree in the triangle. Ginny pulled on the shade's cord, raising it even higher, and perched herself on the wide-edged windowsill noticing the lopsided star at each tree's top. Children laughed and spun and weaved and bobbed between the trees like amateur boxers in a ring, often slipping on the snow that had gathered from flakes that were now as fat as a Christmas goose, nearing the forecast of four to six inches by morning.

White Christmas was playing on TCM, and Ginny, without even being aware, began to hum along to "Sisters," until the reel in her head started to replay so many years spending time with her own sisters, until they became estranged from one another, each recognizing the line that had been crossed and that could never again be erased. Ginny shook her head deliberately and jumped up from the windowsill, found a box of matches, and lit a scattering of candles that invoked memories of holly berry and citrus and moss, pine, spruce, balsam, and cedar. The stove's timer showed that the freshly baked chocolate chip cookies with bits of pecans would be ready in the time it would take her to reheat leftover turkey and stuffing, mashed potatoes, and green beans almondine that she had prepared yesterday.

Before dusk began its descent and the dark night set in, the lights in the eye-level apartment across the street appeared, and its sole inhabitant stood in front of his line-up of pine trees, each with a single strand of multi-colored lights reflecting sparks of intermittent brightness. Ginny's own small, antique, German spindly feather tree seemed rather awkward in its bare simplicity. Still, its dull, tiny, mercury orbs held their own allure, as Ginny remembered Christmases past when it took center stage on her family's fireplace mantel, the crackling logs both lulling her to sleep and keeping her awake to all the magic that the season promised. Ginny sat back down on the windowsill and admired the ornate, heavy, Deco trim along the top of the building's edge, particularly the cobalt blue, repeat wave pattern. She closed her eyes to recall winters spent in the Lowcountry with her husband and her family, each of them wrapped up in coats and scarves and gloves, braving the stinging winds along the pristine beach. Again, she shook her head in a desperate attempt to move past what she could not bring into the present.

The oven's timer buzzed, and she hopped up from her perch, grabbed a mitt, opened the oven door, and breathed in the scent of vanilla, cinnamon, and chocolate, as she grabbed quick bites from her dinner plate, the gravy smooth and buttery. As she moved the cookies to the cooling racks, the tears took their time making their way down her cheek, each one landing softly on the kitchen counter, imitating each fallen snowflake as it landed on the outside edge of her window.

Her neighbor across the street stood, admiring his personal forest of pine trees, raising his arm occasionally to drink what looked like the milky liquid of a Baileys on ice. The trees' lights shimmered on the cut-glass facets of the crystal tumbler, and he began to gently sway back and forth, and Ginny longed to know the accompanying music. That was when she noticed that one of his windows was opened just enough to invite a crisp stream of the cold winds. She considered doing the same, and she muted the sounds from the television. And there it was, the comforting and familiar notes of Nat King Cole's "The Christmas Song." She dimmed the apartment lights and, led only by the flickering flames from the gathered candles, began her own solitary dance. As the streetlights came on and illuminated the city's downtown, she continued to sway long after the music had stopped, and her neighbor's lights were extinguished.

When Ginny woke the next morning and raised high the window shades, the city had been blanketed with a snow that had not yet been disturbed, and once again she set herself on the wide berth of the windowsill, like a tabby, gazing in wonderment. Her cell phone startled her, as the sounds of a text made its arrival, up-ending the peace she had held close. It was from a very dear friend who had journeyed with her these past years as she made her way through far too many losses and each one's fierce accompaniment, grief.

Simply seeing his name on her screen made her smile, knowing that some lovely intangible was on its way for her to unwrap like a present covered in shiny foiled paper under the Christmas tree topped with an intricate bow. After exchanging Christmas greetings, Ginny texted him to give her a minute; she had an idea. She took a photo of the building's continuous wave pattern across the street and invited him to write a haiku, knowing full well that poetry—read or written—was not necessarily something that he embraced; still, she hoped that he would allow her this moment to indulge her love of joining one letter to another to form a series of words that together comprised 17 syllables.

"I'll go first," she texted.

Flakes fall at a slant.
Swirl, flit, catch on spindly limbs.
Cobalt waves wink, wail.

And as Ginny read his reply, she laughed uproariously. "That's crazy," he texted. "Exactly what I was going to write." Ginny texted a line-up of laughing emojis, along with tears that now seemed a natural part of her day, and she longed to one day feel their absence, to celebrate their disappearance. Ginny texted, "The ball is in your court, my friend." He responded, "I still need to clap when I say a word out loud to determine how many syllables it has."

"The word excuses has three," Ginny responded.

She no go in snow.
Stays by window and enjoys.
Warm and dry not cold.

And with those 17 syllables, they bid farewell. Ginny gathered a few fictional friends to help her through the day, knowing that they would not—had never—let her down. Sook and Buddy and Queenie, the inseparable characters from Truman Capote's "A Christmas Memory," which Ginny had read with her husband every Christmas until the Christmas arrived when he was no longer with her, even though he had promised her that he would never do that, unless he had no other choice. The story was so deeply a part of their own story, especially one that reminded her of a winter's adventure aboard Amtrak's Cardinal to New Orleans, the snow again falling lightly and at times heavily outside their sleeping compartment, as they enjoyed steaming mugs of jasmine tea and delectable bits of cranberry scones. Ginny closed her eyes and slept, hoping for a sleep deep enough and long enough to remember details that had already become a bit blurred.

It was well after midnight when Ginny woke, the apartment more chilly than when she had fallen asleep earlier. She walked to the thermostat, drawing the down comforter tight around her, and raised the temperature. She had left raised the widow shade, walked over to gaze out at the still, black, early Christmas morning to be comforted by the gathering of decorated firs, a quiet empty street, and a neighbor across the street in his own aloneness. For the briefest of moments, the orange flame from his lit cigarette caught her eye and his filled champagne flute was raised slightly, the lights from his own forest catching the effervescence. He began to tap dance in a modern-day, dapper Fred Astaire resemblance. A slight and surprising giggle emerged from an unfamiliar place, and as it made its way into hearty laughter, Ginny Johnstone slid across her poured concrete floors in her stockinged feet and danced and danced without any accompaniment.

Snowy Gap Christmas

Rebecca Williams Spindler

Joy finished the last sips of her cinnamon mocha. The scent and taste of cinnamon reminded her of home and the diner. The Evergreen Diner was famous for their cinnamon rolls. It was a Friday tradition for Grace and her mother to bake homemade cinnamon rolls. A recipe they kept secret, passed down from Mamaw Landry's Belgian ancestors. There was a write-up once in the *Scott County Virginia Star* about the diner's cinnamon rolls. Word spread during the pandemic, so much so that Grace baked rolls every day of the week! She got a call one day from a celebrity who requested two dozen to be shipped to New York City. Grace wouldn't say who it was for. Faith said the address went to *Good Morning America*. Faith told Joy those rolls helped to keep the lights on during an otherwise very dark time.

Faith.

Sisterly relations were strained and weakened by years and distance between Joy and Faith. What started out as a bond thick as a tow rope was now thin as a thread. Growing up, Faith was such a huge influence on Joy. Her big sister was a mainstay, more so than

Grace. When she was little, Joy depended on Faith and rarely let her big sister out of her sight. Faith was practically Joy's mini-mom. Joy reminisced about the green mossy plot in Williams Holler where their family's metal-roofed, ranch-style home sat. In the woods up from the holler, the sisters played endless hours of hide-and-seek. Faith had no problems finding Joy. Soft hums gave her away every time. She'd always be singing or humming. On the back porch, the sisters would share a bottle of Orange Crush while they'd exchange secrets and divide the loot from raids on their dad's candy stash in his glove compartment.

Dad.

Joy's heart ached for her father, each and every day. She so missed the phone calls they'd have. Christmas was her dad's favorite time of the year. She wanted to give up on her ambitions in Nashville. Dad told her to "hold tight" and "be patient, your day will come." But it was his day, his final day, that came way too soon. After his funeral, Joy couldn't stand to be in Snowy Gap. Too many memories haunted her. The disappointments she had generated in her family and in her hometown made her chest so tight she could barely breathe.

That old familiar shame sent a chill up Joy's spine. *DING! DING!* Joy glanced at her phone. Faith's guilt-trippy texts were relentless and forced Joy to ignore her sister's attempts to get her attention.

As Joy sat alone in the conference room of Boomtown Records, she felt a pang in her heart. The Christmas season was encroaching and brought an inner turmoil of whether Joy belonged back home in Southwest Virginia or should stay attached to her career as a Record Promoter in Music City.

Adam's voice drifted and caused Joy to stir. He barked orders from within his office, audible for all to hear. Adam was the leather-clad former rocker from the 1980s turned CEO of Boomtown.

"I want the best roadies! Get me Garth's manager on the phone. He had the best teamsters driving his trucks and rigging his tour." Latrice, Boomtown's office queen, stood in Adam's office doorway and noted his demands.

As Joy typed and clicked on her laptop, a FaceTime call came from Audra, the lead singer of Boomtown's emerging star band, Acceleration. Joy grabbed her phone and answered. Audra's nervous face appeared on Joy's phone screen.

"Hey!" Joy answered. "How's it going?"

"JOY! I need your expertise, please! Can't decide what to wear for tonight's interview on iHeartRadio." Audra, a fiery redhead in flowy boho, stepped back. A barrage of clothes on her bed came into view. Joy could sense Audra was on the verge of panic. As Audra paced in her cramped bedroom, Ty, Audra's brother and Acceleration's hunky drummer with bulging biceps, appeared and swung a playful slug to his sister's arm.

"I told her she could rock a burlap sack and nobody'd care!" Ty joked. Audra elbow-jabbed her brother.

"I didn't ask for your opinion, did I? Get on outta here! Let me talk to Joy. ALONE!"

Joy witnessed Audra shove Ty out of view, and the bedroom door slammed. The sibling tantrum reminded Joy of all the ruckus she and Faith would get into. Audra ran a nervous hand through her long hair. "As I was saying. Help!"

Joy peered through the phone screen and spotted a lacy purple silk shirt on Audra's bed. "Purple shirt, black jeans. Remember to breathe and try to glance at the camera once in a while. The audience loves that."

"I don't mind radio interviews. But when it comes to being on camera, I get a bellyful of butterflies and jitters."

"You got this," Joy reassured Audra. She understood fully the fear involved with being up on stage. Being a singer was one thing. Being a performer was something entirely different. *What was it her boyfriend used to say before she took the stage at Dollywood? Oh yeah.* "*Look the part, be the part!*"

Audra held up the purple shirt, and Joy gave her a toothy grin and a thumbs-up.

"Thank you, Joy. You're one helluva Promotions Manager!"

"At your service!" beamed Joy.

Audra sat on the edge of the bed, and Joy could see she had an expression of seriousness. "Have you shared any of your song lyrics with Adam?"

Joy jolted, and her eyes darted to the conference room door. She popped up and went to close the door. "No! I only shared those with you." Joy's voice was barely a whisper.

"Well, I loved 'em, and so did Ty. I think we'll want to add at least a couple of 'em to our next album."

"You can't be serious!" Joy was stunned.

"As a heart attack!" added Audra as she leaned in close to her phone's camera. "You gotta get your name on the books like a real-for-real songwriter."

"Someday maybe. Meanwhile, I've already got a real job. And I happen to enjoy it!" Joy was intense in her answer.

"All right, I won't push ya. But I don't think these songs should be stuck in some ol' notebook. You're sitting on songs that could become gold records. Just sayin'." Audra shrugged.

"I appreciate your sentiment, I do," replied Joy. Audra's comment lit a fire in Joy. Latrice opened the conference room door. Joy glanced up to acknowledge her. "I gotta run. No worries about the interview. You'll be awesome tonight. I'll be listening." Joy smiled with hope. "Bye."

"Buh-bye," Audra said and ended the call.

Latrice, in her long, green peacoat, was ready to go, and she motioned for Joy. "Time to do some shopping. There's a cute Christmas gift shop around the corner."

* * *

Christmas decorations and holiday lights adorned the streetlamps and business windows of Music Row. Latrice looked up and marveled at the festive scenery as she and Joy walked along.

"I just love Christmas! Don't you?" exclaimed Latrice.

"I used to," Joy answered, her gaze focused downward.

"Get in the holiday spirit, doll," Latrice nudged Joy. "Did you get on that dating site I showed you?"

"Not into dating at that moment," Joy grimaced.

"Single and fierce. I'm in that camp too. But it sure would be nice to spend the holidays with someone special."

"I suppose. But I need to concentrate on work and Acceleration's busy schedule." Joy checked her watch. "We need to keep this trip to 30 minutes."

"Guess we'd better pick up the pace!" Latrice clutched her purse tight as she and Joy challenged each other to a power-walk pace. This sporting rivalry created giggles from these friends as they strutted up to a charming holiday boutique, All Things Christmas.

Joy grabbed the door handle and held it open for Latrice. The aroma of peppermint, pine, and Wassail gave a warm welcome to shoppers. Displays and shelves with ornaments, decorations, stuffed animals, holiday-themed housewares, and clothing filled the space.

At a small table near the front counter sat a little old lady in a fuzzy, knitted poncho. On the table were stacks of paper cups and two large carafes—one marked "Cocoa" and the other marked "Wassail." The old lady gave a pleasant smile to customers as they browsed. Latrice hovered at a holiday clothing display and waved over Joy.

"My niece will love these," commented Latrice as she held up a pair of festive mittens.

"I think I'll get a pair for my niece too," Joy murmured.

"So, you're thinking about going back home for Christmas?"

"Maybe. I haven't quite decided yet. I think my family would be okay if I saw them after New Year's. Have to keep a close watch on the Acceleration website for the Christmas Day song drop and all."

"How long has it been since you've been home?" Latrice bobbed her head until she fell into Joy's line of vision.

"I don't know, nine months, maybe?" Joy avoided eye contact with Latrice. She wanted to avoid the question altogether.

"You're putting your entire life on the line for this job, aren't you?" Latrice didn't judge; her words came from heartfelt concern.

"I need to prove my worth to Adam. More than anything, I've got to be successful at this job. I need a win." Joy was surprised by the way her voice cracked and the wetness that formed in her eyes. She turned away from Latrice and stepped over to one of several Christmas trees in the shop, peppered with sparkling ornaments. Cautiously, Latrice followed her and spoke in a hushed and comforting tone.

"Putting a career before your loved ones will only leave you sad and lonely. Go home this Christmas, and maybe it'll help you achieve that win you're so badly seeking."

"I wish going home was as easy as it sounds, but it's not. Unfortunately..." Joy checked her watch and quickly plucked a couple of ornaments off the Christmas tree to add to her purchases. "I need to get back to the office."

Latrice gave a long exhale and proceeded after Joy. Latrice knew how stubborn and hyper-focused Joy could be when it came to her career at Boomtown. An angel ornament caught Joy's attention, and she nabbed it off a Christmas tree. She and Latrice collected their gift items and proceeded to the front counter.

Ahead of them was a man in a black wool coat. Joy's attention was drawn to his neatly groomed chestnut hair. He paid for his purchases and then stepped over to the table where the old woman sold beverages.

"I'll take a hot cocoa, please," said the man. "Could I get it with a dash of cinnamon?"

"Hmpf! Another oddball who likes cinnamon," Latrice whispered to Joy.

Joy perked at the man's request. *Wait, could it be?* Joy leaned to one side as she tried to get a better glimpse of the man's face. He exchanged cash for the cocoa, and just as he turned to leave, Joy tilted too far and bumped into him. He juggled the cocoa and averted a spill.

"Chris?! It *is* you!" Joy squeaked. His handsomeness sucked out all her breath.

"Joy!" Chris replied with elation as he recognized Joy.

For a split second, the years were wiped away. Chris and Joy found each other back in the halls of Snowy Gap High School. This unexpected reunion astounded them.

Latrice noticed the sensational aura these two shared. "Ahem."

The pair broke their magnetized gaze.

"Oh! Latrice, this is Chris. He's a…an…We…" Joy stuttered.

"Hello, nice to meet you." Latrice offered her hand.

Chris juggled the drink and his shopping bag in order to extend an open hand. They had a friendly handshake. "Joy and I go way back. Grew up in Snowy Gap together," answered Chris.

"Uh-huh," Latrice's eyes measured him up. His broad shoulders squared off his fine stature, and those brown eyes of his were deep chocolate pools worth drowning in. His gleaming white smile and firm handshake made him Grade-A stock in Latrice's book.

Joy also stood frozen, taking in his presence. This man was a *man*! Chris was no longer the high school boy who accompanied her to Dollywood and invaded her dreams, especially after she drank too much Jack and Coke. Joy composed herself and suppressed her impulse to reach out and touch him. *Was he really standing right there?*

"What're you doing in Nashville?" Joy blurted out. She couldn't resist the ask.

"Radio broadcaster's conference," he replied. Then he held up the gift bag. "And doing a little Christmas shopping." He flashed that amazing smile of his, which sent tingles up Joy's spine.

The merchant behind the counter grew impatient as Joy and Latrice held up the line of customers who waited to pay for their purchases. Latrice got the hint and presented her gift selections.

"You still work at the radio station?" Joy continued.

"I own the radio station," Chris replied. "Dad retired."

"Wow! That's great, Chris! Give my congrats to your dad. And your mom?"

"She's still working. Not ready to take on Dad full-time," Chris quipped with a smirk. "A lot's happened in Snowy Gap. Have you talked to Faith lately?"

"Yeah, all the time," Joy lied. She was stunned by how fast the lie blew from her lips. Sweet Jesus brought swift justice as Joy's phone chimed, *DING! DING!* "That's probably my boss," Joy lied again and suddenly felt heat rise to her cheeks. Somewhere in Snowy Gap, Faith's ears were burning. "Good to see you, Chris." Finally, Joy spoke a truth.

"You too, Joy. Merry Christmas."

"Merry Christmas," Joy replied.

She watched him turn and walk to the shop's door. Her eyes were glued to his back. At the door, he paused and glanced over his shoulder. She didn't move a muscle and instead let herself be captured in his gaze. They shared a smile and a teensy, yet undeniable spark.

"Your high school flame," probed Latrice.

"Is it that obvious?" Joy asked innocently.

"Does Santa have a beard?" Latrice clamored.

Joy spread her Christmas gifts onto the front counter and handed her credit card to the merchant. The shop door jingled and signaled his departure. Joy watched fondly as Chris passed by the shop's window.

"Maybe I'll head home for Christmas," Joy murmured.

"What'd ya say?" Latrice's head was craned as she watched Chris strut away.

"I think Mama and Faith need me back in Snowy Gap for the holidays."

"Hmm... They're not the only ones who'd appreciate seeing ya." Latrice flashed a jovial wink at Joy. A wide smile curled Joy's lips. The youthful bliss of Christmas found its way back into her heart—and it felt like home.

Our Christmas Tree

Phyllis W. Stevenson

P eggy Sue, I'm cold," said Oliver. "Let's go home."

"Not yet, Oliver, not until we've found the perfect tree," she answered.

"But we've been out here forever," whined Oliver, lagging behind as they made their way farther up the rocky hillside where little grew but Johnson grass and scraggly Virginia Pines.

"Look, I see one," she'd say, and off they'd go. They trudged up and down the hill checking out every tree that looked promising—pines, mostly, and cedars—only to be disappointed upon closer inspection. It wasn't symmetrical, not full enough for Peggy Sue, and too lopsided for ornaments.

In the Southwest Virginia countryside of the 1950s, Peggy Sue had not heard of one Christmas tree farm, not a "store-bought" Christmas tree of any kind. People just took their hatchet or saw, and after getting permission from the landowner (and sometimes not), they headed for the woods. Today, Peggy Sue and Oliver had set out with a purpose. The land was rented by their grandfather, where he grazed his milk cow and grew a few crops. She had brought along Grandpa's smallest handsaw and a little hatchet.

The December day had begun with a hint of "watery" sunlight from the east and a threatening bank of darker clouds from the west—snow clouds. But it wasn't too cold for this time of year.

School had let out the day before, not resuming again till after New Year's. Since Peggy was in the fifth grade, she would be taking mid-term exams for the first time when she returned in January. She planned to use the time after Christmas to really study hard. Having done well on sixth-week tests, she wanted to get a good grade. But a whole mid-term seemed scary.

The fifth grader wasn't concerning herself with that today, for she and her brother were off to find their prize! The most beautiful tree in the forest. At least, the most beautiful one they were able to cut down and lug home. The whole of Christmas depended on the tree! Peggy Sue couldn't put it into words, but the ten-year-old somehow believed that if she and Oliver were good children, tried hard, did their best, and presented Santa Claus (whose existence she was starting to doubt) with a pretty tree, the rest was up to him. My goodness, Santa could even take his pick of the four chimneys they had in that drafty old farmhouse she and Oliver shared with Mother and their grandparents. Their daddy had died a few years earlier.

Their warm breakfast of oatmeal and hot cocoa was long forgotten. Peggy Sue wouldn't admit it to Oliver, but she was hungry.

"But I'm really hungry, Peggy Sue," moaned Oliver.

"It won't be much longer now, Oliver, and I promise if we don't find one soon, we'll head home." Peggy Sue remained optimistic. Somebody had to.

She hadn't noticed that daylight was fading behind a dark

cloud. The wind had picked up. Snow flurries were beginning to land on their heads and coats. No wonder Oliver was cold. She pulled his cap down over his ears, buttoned his coat and tightened her scarf around her neck, and adjusted her earmuffs. Neither child, in their haste to leave the house, had remembered their gloves nor mittens. Their hands were cold.

At the top of a hill, both of them stopped and spied the same tree. They stood beside it in awe. The tree was a little taller than Peggy Sue and full and perfectly symmetrical. It was indeed the most beautiful little cedar tree there ever was!

"Okay, Oliver, what do you think?"

"I like it, now can we chop it down and go home?" asked the hungry five-year-old.

The earth was hard and cold on her knees, but she didn't care. Peggy Sue went to sawing at the trunk of that little tree just a few inches above the ground. It was harder than she thought it would be.

"Little tree, you're going to be even prettier when we get you home," Peggy Sue said.

It took all the effort she had to push and pull that saw. Her hands hurt.

"Hand me that hatchet, Oliver," she gasped. With a couple of whacks, finally, the little cedar released its tie to the Virginia hillside and fell to the ground.

Relieved and with their prize, they headed home. It was the Winter Solstice, the shortest day of the year, and darkness would fall soon. Peggy Sue was tired. She dragged the tree for a while, then she let Oliver drag it a little way just to feel he'd been part of the effort, too. They were cold, hungry, and proud, for this was the first time she and Oliver had been able to go alone without an adult to cut the tree. It was a big deal for them.

The children and their beautiful tree made tracks in the snow, which was coming down in big, soft flakes, and finally made it home. They left the tree on the back porch and called everyone to come see!

After supper, Grandpa found a wooden board. He sawed it in two places, then nailed them crosswise. The board held the tree upright, and he made sure it wouldn't topple over.

"Well, lass, you sure found yourself a good tree there," Grandpa said, patting Peggy Sue on the top of her head. "I'm surprised you were able to get it down."

"Me too," replied Peggy Sue, and she proudly showed him her blistered hands.

It was so good to feel warm and have bellies full of Granny's good biscuits, but nothing would deter the children. They had to decorate the tree tonight! Immediately, Oliver wanted to throw silvery icicles on it. That was his favorite thing to do. Peggy Sue explained that would come later. First, they were going to make garlands. Momma and Peggy Sue showed Oliver how to make them out of green and red construction paper while Granny set to popping popcorn in hot oil on the old-fashioned wood stove. Grandpa made sure there was plenty of wood on hand and brought in extra for Granny. With the coming snow, he made sure there was a good supply of dry wood stacked high on the back porch.

When the popcorn cooled, Peggy Sue began stringing the white, puffy kernels with a needle and thread. Oliver was supposed to be helping, handing her the kernels, but they kept disappearing.

"Oliver, stop eating the garland!" she yelled.

"I'm sorry, Peggy Sue, it just smells so good. I couldn't help it."

Granny obliged by popping another kettle just for eating. The smell of fresh popcorn filled the entire house. The radio played Christmas carols, and soon the children were singing along to "Up on the Housetop."

Finally, the garlands were finished. After the popcorn string and paper garland were carefully placed on the tree by Peggy Sue, next came the red glass balls Momma had bought the year after Daddy died. Momma had saved her money from working at the shirt factory in town. She surprised Peggy Sue and Oliver one Christmas Eve after they returned home with Grandpa and Granny from the Christmas Eve church service. They arrived home to find a beautifully decorated Christmas tree with presents all around.

"Ole Sannie's been here," Momma proclaimed. "And look what he left you!"

There was a chalkboard for Peggy Sue with her name printed on top of the wooden frame. That became Peggy Sue's first memory of Christmas. Oliver was only a toddler, so he probably didn't remember anything.

Now it was Oliver's turn to place a treasured ball on the fat little cedar tree. Momma's box of glass balls started with 12 that first year, but only eight remained. Each year, seemingly at least one fell as a casualty. Oliver carefully slipped the ribbon of the ornament over a tree branch, and the precious glass ball stayed put.

"Look, Peggy Sue, look Momma, look Grandpa!" Grandpa turned his attention from smoking his pipe at the fire to the tree. "See how pretty it is," Oliver continued, "and I didn't drop it, either." The happy little boy grinned.

Next came the icicles, and Oliver tossed them surprisingly one strand at a time. What control for such a small boy. Perhaps, he wanted the moment to last. Peggy Sue had something new and special to share with her brother. Her Aunt Marie had given her some "angel hair." She waited until Oliver was done with his icicles. Peggy Sue gave him some angel hair and showed him how to drape it on the tree.

"Is this really angel hair, Sissy?" he asked.

"I don't know what real angel hair looks like. But it sure is pretty," replied Peggy Sue.

Eventually, their project was finished. The children backed away and called to the family to come see, and everyone agreed that it did look just like a magical tree in the forest on Christmas Eve. With that, Peggy Sue and Oliver were ushered off to bed after a very long, tiring, yet happy day.

After the children had gone off to bed, the grownups mumbled, "Getting so worked up over a Christmas tree when there's not going to be much under it come Christmas morning."

Christmas Eve had arrived, and earlier that day, men had come from the forest with a sled pulled by a farmer's big horse. The sled was loaded with evergreens and holly to decorate the church sanctuary. Peggy Sue's Uncle Ed was one of those men.

When people arrived that evening at church, they were greeted by a beautiful scene. A large holly wreath topped with a red bow hung on the front door. Inside, candles and greenery had been placed on every windowsill. The single-room church was filled with the aroma of cedars, pines, balsams, and candle wax.

This year, it was Peggy Sue who had been appointed the reader of the Christmas Eve story. For weeks, she'd been going around the house reciting her lines out loud so that even Oliver had learned some of them. After all were seated, the lights were turned off. Someone lit a large candle at the top of the sanctuary. Peggy Sue, covered in a white choir robe, knelt down and began to recite the story of the "heavenly babe wrapped in swaddling clothes in a manger laid…"

The sanctuary was very still, and all eyes had been on Peggy Sue as she flawlessly recited her piece. After she finished, Peggy Sue took her seat in the pew with the family. Next came Oliver and a little group of children consisting mostly of his cousins who stood and sang "Away in a Manger." Oliver looked straight ahead, his blond hair parted to one side and blue eyes shining. After the children's song, the organist launched into "Silent Night," and everyone stood and sang every verse. The minister closed with a prayer. Service was over, and the lights came back on. Many grown-ups came up to Peggy Sue and Oliver and told them how well they had done. Soon, everyone left the warmth of the church and headed home. Most folks lived within walking distance, and it was a treat to get to walk home on Christmas Eve with a bright moon and a sky full of stars. Oliver pointed up.

"Do you think that's the Star of Bethlehem, Grandpa?" he asked. "The same one the Wise Men followed?"

"Probably was, laddie, probably was," Grandpa replied.

They walked home happily, talking about the evening program and Santa's arrival later that night. Each child carried a bag of candy, nuts, and fruit they'd been handed when leaving church. Tomorrow would be Christmas Day!

Grandpa had gotten up early and made a warm fire in the big fireplace. He peeked a second time into Peggy Sue's and Oliver's stockings to make sure the little homemade basket and slingshot he had made were in their rightful places. The aroma of fresh, fried apple pies, biscuits, and sausage gravy filled the air. Granny and Momma spoke in soft voices so as not to let the children hear.

Oliver was the first one out of bed and woke Peggy Sue. They hurried in to see what Santa Claus had brought them, first checking their stockings by the fireplace. Peggy Sue found the basket, which could be used to store crayons or pencils. Oliver found his slingshot. Oliver was a little young for a slingshot, but he'd learn.

The children rushed to the Christmas tree. The grownups were right; there wasn't a lot left under that pretty tree. Peggy Sue began to wonder, *Had Santa made some kind of mistake?* Maybe Santa checked his list and...Peggy Sue didn't sass her elders and only teased her brother a little bit. Oliver hadn't been all that perfect, but good grief! There were only four presents total under that tree. Two gifts for each child.

Peggy Sue unwrapped her presents to find three pairs of panties and two pairs of socks. Oliver faired a little better with a flannel shirt and a tiny toy truck. Peggy Sue's mind reeled...*Had something happened to Santa? Did he have a wreck somewhere between the North Pole and their house?* Peggy Sue stayed quiet the rest of the day and kept her thoughts and disappointments to herself.

When the stores opened up after the holidays, Uncle Ed, Momma's brother, who was still single and lived at home, put on his warm coat and walked the three miles into town. He returned later that day with a beautiful baby doll with big blue eyes, golden curls that you could comb, and skin as smooth as a real baby's. All this was topped off with a pretty, pink, silky dress; petticoat; pink socks; and white shoes. Oliver was thrilled with the Radio Flyer wagon Uncle Ed brought him. Uncle Ed had saved Christmas. All evening, the children played with their new toys.

Uncle Ed was illiterate and nearsighted, and he could only find work as a day laborer. What money he had earned, he'd spent on Christmas gifts for his niece and nephew. Peggy Sue held on to that baby doll all through high school, long past the time kids played with toys. Peggy Sue would always love her uncle for what he had done.

The Santa Claus Special

Mary Woodside

November 2002
Kingsport, Tennessee

My hands shake as I fumble with the zipper. Sadie comes behind me and wraps her arms around my waist. "Let me," she says.

I turn to face her and, with a voice every bit as shaky as my hands, remark, "I didn't think I'd be this nervous. Feels like our wedding day all over again."

Sadie grabs the trim of my coat, pushes onto her toes, and plants a firm kiss on my lips. It's the kind of kiss that holds 40 years of life, love, and loss; history and memories, arguments and reconciliation, and choosing each other again and again. "You were a lot of things on our wedding day," she grins, "but nervous was not one of them."

I smile at the memory. "All the same, I wish you were coming with me tomorrow."

"Tomorrow is your day," Sadie says. "Maybe next year I'll join you."

She spins me around to face the mirror, and for the first time, I see myself in the full suit. My breath catches, and my eyes sting. Matthew Parker is long gone. Staring back at me is the likeness of the man who saved my life 59 years ago. "Pretty convincing," I say with a wry chuckle. Then, in a whisper, "I just hope I do him justice."

"You will," Sadie assures me. "You will."

* * *

November 1943
Fort Blackmore, Virginia

1943 was a year we were happy to see the back of. The same could be said of 1942…and 1941…and truthfully, every other year I'd been alive. But 1943—it was a real doozy. Folks in the mountains had never quite climbed out of the Depression. Places with more industry fared better once America entered the war, but in the mountains, we still had sallow eyes and hungry bellies.

The previous winter, my little sister, Helen, got so weak from sickness and hunger that one day, she couldn't climb out of bed. Daddy stalked out of the house that morning, and when he came home at nightfall, he carried an armful of groceries and a wad of dollar bills.

"Where'd you get that?" Mama asked.

"Uncle Sam," Daddy answered, not looking at her.

Helen and I heard the two of them arguing that night when they thought we were asleep. We didn't mean to eavesdrop, but with their bed just steps away from the one Helen and I shared, it was inevitable.

"We can find another way, Frank."

"I'll not watch my daughter waste away," Daddy said. "The Army'll pay me $150 a month. $150, Corrie! We ain't seen money like that in over a decade. And besides, it's done now. There's no going back on Uncle Sam."

He was right. There was no going back. The day my daddy walked out the door was the last time I ever saw him. A Purple Heart that sits on the mantle is all that's left of Frank Parker.

After Daddy died, Mama did her best to keep the farm going. Uncle Sam was supposed to send a survivor's pension to care for Mama and us kids, but I suppose it went missing along with Daddy's body. Mama took in sewing whenever she could, but it never seemed to be enough. Finally, the first week of November, she sat me and Helen down on the edge of the bed and delivered the news.

"I've decided to go to Kingsport for a spell. We need money, and if I can find work that pays…" Her words trailed off, but she didn't need to say them. I knew. If Mama could find work that paid, we would have no more dinners of watered-down mashed potatoes. If Mama could find work that paid, we could get medicine to keep Helen's cough away for good. If Mama could find work that paid, we could buy cloth and shoes and fuel and seed and 50 other things we needed but couldn't afford. Heck, if Mama could find work that paid, we could sell the farm, move to Kingsport, and start a new life. It would mean cutting ties to our life with Daddy, but if you've ever gone hungry, you know that sentimentality is a poor companion to an empty stomach.

If Mama could find work that paid…

* * *

The day Mama left was sunny, warm, and full of promise. "Matthew," she said, smoothing down an unruly clump of my hair, "look after your sister while I'm gone. And the farm, of course. There's a post on the pasture fence that needs to be replaced, and the winter squash should be ripe soon. If I'm not back, Mrs. Carter will help y'all can it. She'll look in on you every few days."

I nodded solemnly as Mama listed each item that needed tending to, though none of the information was new. We'd been running this farm together since Daddy joined up, and I knew every inch of it just as well as she did, maybe better.

"I sure wish I didn't have to leave such a heavy burden on your shoulders, Matty boy," Mama said with a deep sigh.

I straightened up to my full height and swatted her hand off my hair. "I can handle it, Mama. I'm not a boy anymore. I can take care of us and the farm, too."

"I know you can," she said with a sad smile. "I just wish you didn't have to."

I pulled Helen close to my side as Mama walked away. She buried her face in my chest and tried not to cry, but I felt her shoulders quivering all the same. "I've got a good feeling about this," I told her. "Things are finally gonna turn around for us. You'll see, Helen. You'll see."

She said nothing, but I didn't expect her to. She hadn't spoken a word since the telegraph came. "It's my fault," she'd sputtered through a flood of tears. "He did it because of me." Mama shushed and soothed, but to no avail. Helen's guilt had weighed down her tongue ever since.

It was quiet after Mama left. I missed the way she hummed and sang while doing chores. I missed her prayers over our food, our farm, and our family. But mostly I just missed her and the comfort of her presence.

Things started out well for Helen and me. The squash came in, and I caught two rabbits in one of Daddy's old traps. We ate better that first week than we had in months. But there was no word from Mama. We tried to stay busy, but then another week passed with still no word. By the third week, we were constantly looking out windows or over our shoulders. We hoped to high heaven we'd see her form walking down the road, but the road was as empty as ever.

* * *

"There's a storm blowin' in tonight," Mrs. Carter told us one evening on her way home from the general store. "I suspect it'll be a bad one by the way my animals are behaving. Do you two need anything?"

"No," I lied. "The barn's secure, and my traps are performing well. Just need to chop up some firewood and the two of us will be fine." The truth was that the barn door had a broken hinge, my traps hadn't caught anything since those two rabbits, and the ax handle was broken, meaning there wouldn't be any more firewood. But Mrs. Carter didn't need to know that. She had six children at home and a husband off at war; she didn't need two more mouths to feed.

Mama would be home soon, and Helen and I would be okay until then. At least that's what I told myself. And every time the barn door banged in the wind, I told myself again. And when all we had to eat was broth and a corn cake, I repeated the words again still. And as Helen and I shivered under threadbare quilts with only a smoldering fire to warm us, I said the words aloud, for both her sake and mine. But when Helen woke in the morning with a deep, wet cough that just wouldn't quit, I stopped saying the words.

* * *

Mrs. Carter was right about the storm; it was a bad one. Five inches of snow and ice fell on our farm, and the temperature turned bitterly cold. That much snow so early in the season didn't bode well for winter—and didn't bode well for us. Every time I heard Helen cough, guilt stabbed my heart. Why had I been so stubborn and prideful yesterday when Mrs. Carter offered to take us in? I had to make things right. I promised Mama I would take care of Helen, and I wouldn't break my word.

"We can't stay here another night," I told Helen. "I'll clear us a path to the Carter place, and if Mrs. Carter'll still have us, we'll stay there till Mama comes back."

A look of fear crossed Helen's face, and I knew what she was thinking. If something happened to me, she'd be all alone, and if she were all alone...I shuddered, unable to finish the thought. "Nothing will happen to me," I promised her, and I prayed to God that the words were true.

I pulled on the pair of boots next to the door. We all shared one pair. They used to belong to Daddy, so Helen and I stuffed them with rags or leaves or whatever else was lying around. But that day, I didn't dare take anything that might be of use to Helen, not even the dingiest rag, so my feet just flopped around in the oversized shoes.

The Carter place was less than half a mile from ours, but it was slow going with all the snow. I took an old shovel from the barn and dragged it along in my wake, making a way for Helen. I knew she would struggle to get up Chestnut Ridge, but once at the top, she could practically slide down the other side.

When I saw the Carter farm and the plume of smoke escaping

from their chimney, it seemed like a hundred-pound weight lifted from my chest and floated away with the ash. I almost broke into a run—or what passed for a run in so much snow. But as I approached the house, Mrs. Carter flung open the door and yelled, "STOP! Don't come any closer, Matthew Parker!"

"Mrs. Carter? What's the matter?"

"It's Gordon," she sobbed. "Tuberculous. Must've picked it up in the factory."

Gordon was Mrs. Carter's oldest son. After Mr. Carter enlisted, Gordon, just 15, took a job at Eastman and provided indispensable help to his mother. I didn't like to think about how the family would get on without his income. "Oh, Mrs. Carter! I'm so sorry," I said. "Is there anything I can do to help?"

"No, boy, you just don't come any closer. I don't want you taking this back to your sister. And heaven knows you have enough on your plate with your mama gone."

The walk back home was one of the longest of my life. My steps were slow and plodding as I tried to come up with another plan. The Carters were our closest neighbors. About three-quarters of a mile on the far side of our farm was the Huffman place. The Huffmans were an older couple. They'd never had children and usually kept to themselves. Still, in a pinch, they would probably take us in, and this was a pinch like I'd never been in before.

I mentally calculated how long it would take to get to their house from the Carters. I wouldn't have time to blaze a path for Helen. If we were going to make it before dark, she would have to come with me the first time. I picked up my pace now that I had renewed purpose, but just as I got to the top of Chestnut Ridge, the weather turned again. Big, fat flakes of snow came swirling from the sky. I froze in my tracks and turned my face upward, begging the snow to stop. When it didn't, I sank to my knees and began to cry.

I'm not sure how long I sat there. Long enough to start shaking. I would've sat there even longer if not for the singing. At first, I thought I'd gone crazy, except that the melody kept getting louder.

Jolly old Saint Nicholas,
Lean your ear this way;
Don't you tell a single soul
What I'm going to say.

"Why, hello there!" shouted an overly cheerful voice.

I looked up, and two men stood before me. The one who had been singing extended an arm and helped me to my feet. He had kind eyes and a gentle way about him. His companion was a little younger and spoke next. "Looks like we're gonna get some more snow! Probably because old Santa Claus is coming to town!"

I gave the man a puzzled expression, and he handed me a flyer. "The Santa Claus Special?" I read aloud.

"That's right!" he said. "The big man himself is coming through and catching a ride on our very own Clinchfield Railroad!"

I didn't have time for seasonal merrymaking, so I handed the flyer back without a word.

"Don't tell me you're too old for Santa Claus!" said the first jolly man.

"Just don't have much use for him, I suppose. He can't bring me what I need, so what's the point?"

"And what do you need, son?" asked the second man with concern.

"I need a new ax handle, some dry firewood, food, medicine for Helen, and—" I paused as my bottom lip began to tremble. "Mama.

What I really need is Mama. But Santa Claus can't bring me that."

The second man bent down, put a hand on my shoulder, and whispered, "Ole Santa sees you, boy. You can be sure of it."

I dried my eyes and, at the men's request, let them accompany me back home. They took one look around our house, exchanged a grave look, then the first man said, "I know we just met, but I'd like the pair of you to come home with me for a few days."

Helen looked at me like an animal caught in a trap. The man must have seen her panic because he quickly added, "Just until we find your mama, of course. You said she'd gone to Kingsport to look for work, and that happens to be where I live. John, too," he gestured to the second man. "The name's Joe Higgins, by the way. My wife, Clara, and I would be happy to have you stay with us. And we have some excellent doctors who could listen to your cough, Helen."

Helen was still wide-eyed, so I took her hand and whispered in her ear, "We have to, Helen. We have to go." A single tear slipped from her eyes, and she gave an almost imperceptible nod. "Thank you, sir," I said resolutely. "We're much obliged." And with those little words, Helen and I were bound for Kingsport just like Mama. As I closed the door to our little house, I couldn't help wondering when—or if—any of us would be back

* * *

The days we spent in Kingsport were some of the busiest and best we'd had since Daddy died. Mr. Higgins and Mr. John Dudney, the second man from Chestnut Ridge, belonged to a group of Kingsport businessmen organizing the Santa Claus Special. On the Saturday before Thanksgiving, Santa Claus would ride the

Clinchfield Railroad through parts of Kentucky, Virginia, and Tennessee and deliver presents to boys and girls. Helen and I quickly joined the ranks of "elves" preparing for his trip. I helped mix and wrap hard candy while Helen—Mrs. Higgins being mindful of her cough—stayed home and sewed dolls for the little girls. It felt good knowing our work would bring joy to other children, and the long hours kept our minds off Mama and the fact that Mr. Higgins still hadn't found her.

The night before the event, the train carrying Santa and his gifts would leave Kingsport so it could get an early start at Shelby Yard, Kentucky, the following morning. Mrs. Higgins escorted Helen and me to the train station to see it off.

"Where's Mr. Higgins?" I asked. The station was bustling with activity, and Mr. Higgins was usually right in the thick of it. That night, however, he was nowhere to be seen.

"Joe had some pressing business to attend to," said Mrs. Higgins with a twinkle. "But don't you worry about him—Santa is the man of the hour tonight!"

When the last car was loaded and the flurry began to wane, the volunteers assembled around the train's caboose. A strange hush settled on the crowd, and I could hear footsteps inside the car. A moment later, the door opened, and the crowd went wild as Santa Claus himself stood on the platform smiling and waving.

"Merry Christmas, Kingsport!" he said with a jolly laugh. "From the bottom of my heart, I want to thank you for helping me make this Christmas special for the boys and girls of our beloved mountains. But there are two young people I want to especially thank. They worked every bit as hard as the adults this week and didn't sneak half as much of the candy!" The crowd laughed and Santa waited for them to quiet. "To show my appreciation," he continued,

"I'd like to invite them to join me on the train tomorrow. Matthew and Helen Parker, come on up here!"

The volunteers cheered and applauded, but Helen and I were rooted in place with shock. It wasn't until Mrs. Higgins gave us a gentle shove that we climbed aboard the train.

Santa turned us to face the crowd, put an arm around each of us, and waited for the noise to die down. "You'll need a parent's permission, of course, before I whisk you away. Should we ask your mother?"

My mouth suddenly went dry, but before I could tell him that Helen and I weren't able to ask Mama, the door behind us opened, and a soft, sweet voice said, "I give my permission, Santa."

I whipped around, and there, with arms outstretched and eyes shining, was—

"Mama!" Helen cried and jumped into her arms.

Time froze as we stood there hugging and crying and laughing. When Santa finally ushered us inside, I noticed tears in his eyes, too.

* * *

November 2002
Shelby Yard, Kentucky

I can hear the crowd outside the station. I close my eyes to savor the moment and send up a quick prayer that I might impact these children's futures the way mine was impacted so long ago. When my fingers touch the cool handle of the door, a thousand memories come flooding back. It took me a full year to realize it was Mr. Higgins underneath that Santa suit. I wasn't disappointed when I found out. In fact, it only made me believe in Santa all the more. Anyone can don a red suit and say, "Ho, Ho, Ho!" Mr. Higgins brought me what I wanted most for Christmas—and even beyond—when he tracked down Mama and got her a job at the newspaper. I reckon that makes him the truest Santa of all.

"For you, Joe," I whisper before stepping onto the platform as Old Saint Nick. As I greet each child with a smile and a present, I tell them the same words that changed my life that day on Chestnut Ridge: "Ole Santa sees you!"

Historical Note

In November 1943, a group of Kingsport businessmen banded together to give back to the children of our region. The legacy they began continues today. On the Saturday before Thanksgiving, the Santa Train—originally the Santa Claus Special—runs through Eastern Kentucky, Southwest Virginia, and East Tennessee, distributing candy and presents to children along the Clinchfield (now CSX) Railroad. Joe Higgins and John Dudney were instrumental in organizing this event and handed out flyers in the communities along the tracks. They also both served tenures as Santa Claus. Dudney famously told the children, "Ole Santa sees you!"

Members of the Parker family are fictional characters not based on any real individuals. Their actions—and interactions with the real-life organizers of the Santa Train—are works of the author's imagination.

About the Authors

Lori C. Byington grew up in Bristol, Va., and is a professor of English composition at King University. She loves to write, bake, teach, and ski with her son. Her other short stories have been included in Jan-Carol Publishing's anthologies throughout the last few years.

Colleen De Simone grew up in East Tennessee with a family that cultivated a life-long love of all things Christmas. As an adult, she enjoys romance writing, poetry, and planning for the holidays all year.

Susan Dickenson lives in Bristol, Va., with her husband and two dogs. Dickenson enjoys spending time with her family, birding, and writing. Her short stories include "Wisteria Blooms and a Hint of Cotillion," included in the anthology *Daffodil Dreams*, and "Her Knight in Flannel Armor" in *Steamy Creek: A Cozy Romance Anthology*. Her poem, "Lavender Fields," is included in The Virginia Writer's Club 2024 Golden Nib and Teen Nib.

April **Hensley** loves writing about nature, people, and life in the Appalachian Mountains. Her stories appear in *These Haunted Hills*, *Self-Rising Flowers*, and *Broken Petals*. She writes a monthly gardening article for *Voice Magazine for Women* and has recently published *Four Seasons: Gardening and Growing in Zone 7*.

Linda Hudson Hoagland, a regional writer from Tazewell, Va., has written many mystery novels along with works of nonfiction, five collections of short writings, and five volumes of poems. She has two grown sons, and she is very proud of both of them.

Jan Howery, a native of Southwest Virginia, writes with an Appalachian influence. Her stories have been included in anthologies *Broken Petals*; *Wild Daisies*; *Scattered Flowers*; *Daffodil Dreams*; and *Steamy Creek: A Cozy Romance Anthology*. Her work has also been featured throughout Jan-Carol Publishing's *These Haunted Hills: A Collection of Short Stories*. Howery's debut novel, *Gone Before Breakfast*, was released in 2023, and her second novel in the *Whisper Cozy Romance Mystery Series, The Last Thing I Remember*, released in 2025. Other writings include fashion and health columns for the Appalachian regional magazine *Voice Magazine for Women* and the online literary magazine *Tapestry Journal: Indie Publishing*.

Kathleen M. Jacobs holds an MA in humanistic studies and is the author of *The Harboring & other stories*. She divides her time between the Appalachian region and New York City. Visit her at www.kathleenmjacobs.com.

Rebecca Williams Spindler is an award-winning author, screenwriter, and producer. As an Asian-Appalachian American, her large, diverse family fuels her content. She's the co-host of the podcast *Faith, Final Drafts and the F Word*. She and her daughter, Madelyn, have created a series of middle grade and YA novels and a forthcoming children's picture book. Rebecca has several screenplay projects in development with a Nashville production company. Find her at www.spindlerwriting.com and www.facebook.com/fansofspindlerwriting.

Phyllis Williams Stevenson is a native of Southwest Virginia. She is a devoted wife, mother, grandmother (Mamoo), sister, aunt, and graduate of Warren Wilson College. She's served as a literacy volunteer for elementary students and as a talented framer and decorator for many years. She was born and raised in Scott County, Va., and holds a deep connection to her Appalachian birthplace.

Mary Woodside is a writer, historian, and emphatic believer in the power of stories. Throughout her career, she has brought stories to life for visitors of museums and historic sites, but she most loves creating stories for her four young children.